Woman With
a Man Inside

WOMAN WITH A MAN INSIDE

◆

BARBARA PARKIN

NIGHTWOOD
EDITIONS

Nightwood Editions
R.R.2 • S.26 • C.3
Gibsons • BC V0N 1V0 • Canada

Edited by Sean Virgo.
Cover art by Giddeon L. Flitt, "The Theft" (1992), oil on linen 79" x 43"; private collection, Hamburg, Germany.
Cover design by Kim LaFave.
Author photograph by Margot Fraser.
Page design & layout by David Lee Communications.
Excerpt from *The Robber Bride* by Margaret Atwood © 1993, used by permission of the Canadian Publishers, McClelland & Stewart, Toronto. Excerpt from *mother, not mother* by Di Brandt used by permission of the author and The Mercury Press.
Published with the assistance of the Canada Council.
Printed and bound in Canada.

Canadian Cataloguing in Publication Data

Parkin, Barbara, 1961–
  Woman with a man inside

  ISBN 0-88971-162-3

  I. Title.
PS8581.A76232W65 1996   C813'.54   C96-910571-1
PR9199.3.P345W65 1996

CONTENTS

I ◆ The Room Behind Her

The Room Behind Her 10

II ◆ Woman With a Man Inside

Open Zoo 19
Brochure to Save the Marriage 31
In Hiding 38
Miss Sixteenth 46
In Place of You 59
Belongings 71
Woman With a Man Inside 88

III ◆ Motherland

The Waiting Rooms 107
Philipa of Harare 115
You Are Mine 143

I want to thank the following for their help along the way: Mary Cameron, Cathy Stonehouse, Nick Hughes and Linda Svendsen for readings and advice; my editor Sean Virgo and the people at Nightwood Editions for making this book possible; Keith Maillard, for his early and vital encouragement. Special thanks to my sister Janet Lynn and my parents Mary and Bill for their support and the gift of time. Finally, I thank Mark Cochrane for his belief, insights and the hours spent reading and rereading these stories.

Some of the stories in this book have appeared in earlier forms in the following publications: "The Room Behind Her" and "The Waiting Rooms" in *Room of One's Own*, "Open Zoo" in *Descant* and *Coming Attractions 93*, "Brochure to Save the Marriage" in *Capilano Review* and *The Vancouver Sun*, "In Hiding" in *Canadian Author & Bookman*, "Miss Sixteenth" and "Philipa of Harare" in *Canadian Fiction Magazine*, "In Place of You" and "Belongings" in *Coming Attractions 93*, and "You Are Mine" in *Queen's Quarterly*.

This book was largely written with the financial support of the former Canada Council Explorations Program.

Barbara Parkin

For Mark

I

The Room Behind Her

not-mother,
there's a hole in me

the size of you

Di Brandt
mother, not mother

STEAM FILMS THE CAFE WINDOWS AND runny Vancouver snow streams outside; inside, a beautiful man with a severe haircut makes cafe au lait and pronounces three dollars with some discomfort. This is as close as I'll get to Montreal in the winter time.

I take a table lodged against the wall and read but don't read, only turning pages at random intervals.

The other tables are empty, orderly and still, a small lit candle at the centre of each tablecloth. The ochre walls are flat and don't reflect; it's not easy to see myself.

The man lets music full of horns through the stereo and the sound undrapes things in my head: an ad-man's Everywoman in a breezy white dress, carrying a martini glass, poking at the olive with her sharp manicured nails while the music rises and twists around her. She stands beside the open window overlooking the beach at Monaco, catching the salt wind in her dress. I believe her life is full in the rooms behind her, but what she already possesses is never enough.

Above the door the bell chimes as a woman and a young girl enter, shaking themselves wet, pulling off mittens and toques. As far as I can tell the woman asks for her regular meal—potato soup—in French. The man says there's none. She swears in two languages.

I empathize, but not with her hunger. I'm thinking of the month I bought a box of pads in preparation for the next month, and the next month there was no blood, and the following month—dry. I did not plan in advance for my last time to bleed.

Nor could I have planned for the last time Mother's breast would enter my mouth, offering her perfect food. I pretend I can remember her guiding the nipple to my mouth for the final time, her knowing it would be our last feeding, from body to body. I imagine I lay there sucking, cooing into her chest, carrying on as if it were a meal like any other.

I pretend about my mother, invent scenes between us, rewrite the endings to her many departures. I stop her from leaving me, make her retrace her steps out the door, suddenly whole and recovered, capable of giving herself. I allow her to become something more than ephemeral. She touches my shoulder. I wish the length of her warm fingers was the only measure of the distance between us. Her fingers bring me closer to her body, inviting me in again.

The girl runs a race with herself up and down the length of the cafe. She can sit in her mother's lap or insist on being in her own chair. Either way her mother will be there, and so the girl is free.

Last summer, in a cafe on Rue St. Denis in Montreal, I decided to buy a down-filled coat, to abandon the Pacific for the St. Lawrence. Across from me Carl drank from a bowl, a ring of milk foam around his mouth. I said I would live in the apartment next door to his, but not with him.

Carl said, "It's all or nothing."

I had not been a single woman for long. I could not choose the "all" again, not yet.

Before Carl moved to Montreal, he and I used to walk together in the woods that border the university every Wednesday and Friday after Shakespeare class. The love between my husband and I had been growing smaller and smaller, like a fetus in a gestational video being played in reverse.

I had asked Carl to assist me, to help me cart myself out of the marriage. He agreed. We made love on a bed of ferns and cedar chips during the weeks before he left. He moved to Montreal the day we graduated from university.

Carl wanted it all.

Sometimes I phone him after 11 p.m. when the rates are low and hear a French woman answer, French music in the background. I listen. I drape the coat across my legs, watch my hand press into the pockets of down.

Sad Eric Satie music falls on us, but the mother and daughter play pat-a-cake anyway. The man foaming milk for cafes au lait makes a lot of brief phone calls. He talks to Julia, then dials George. He makes decisions, I can tell. So do the mother and daughter.

They have not said half-way.

You can't push a baby out and say, "Only half-way, please."

The summer I turned seven, my mother left for an indefinite amount of time. I spent much of my day looking for her, for pieces of her. Inside her closet, the hollow wool dresses and jackets held her shape. I squeezed her dresses around the waist, breathing her in, and the arm shapes did not push me back.

I found her in jewelry, stealing her mother-of-pearl brooch to wear on my sweater. Her cameo earrings were clipped secretly on my lobes— the white bust of a woman against blue stone, a hair ribbon floating freely around her face.

That summer, I made her up. She walked down our green lush alley, bright and recovered. Chemicals in harmonious balance. No longer porcelain, no longer a bright smile with glass eyes, no longer a mannequin.

The ripe blackberry bushes reached out at her, inviting her to pick them, to enjoy this small and perfect breath in her life. Her ice-cream bucket swinging in one hand, ready to harvest. Her other arm reaching out to me, Come, darling, let me hold you.

They, my father and my uncles and my aunts, cared for me in her absence. She was a resident at a retreat, they said. To a quiet summer house for a rest. She needed to rest a lot when she was home, too. The aunts took me to the beach and for rides on the train.

Children should not be burdened; children should be allowed to be children; they should not worry, poor girl. *But the hole remained a hole, the unspeakable mystery that was being practiced upon her, somewhere.*

Carl and I could never have been contained by a billboard, exchanging diamond rings on an orangy palm beach. Ad-men don't believe men you screw in the park can eventually become husbands. I blame it on the city. I carry the harbour everywhere, my hollow filled with salt water. When I went to Montreal the smell of sea grass travelled in my knapsack.

I didn't bring Montreal home, no slow-cooked meats or pastries from Rue St. Laurent, although Carl took me there, to buy my coat for the winter we had planned together. I wanted to be near him. I was almost certain we could break the barrier between us, the wall of concrete between our neighboring apartments. I said I would keep my front door open, but he insisted we share the same door, that my door—open or closed—become his, too. Half-way is no way.

I had a landlady who once held the lease on the early years of my first marriage. Bitterness had a hold of her, had shaped her face into a portrait of lines and regret. There is one great love for each of us, one person who can fill us. Take what's yours, Colleen. *She was*

13

wrong, of course. The stale smell of loss around her.

I returned to Vancouver with a discount down coat. On Spanish Banks Beach I held my city in outstretched hands, the West End towers tall in my palm, unconcerned with what might be happening elsewhere. In this temperate place it's possible to live without permanent shelter, without a lease.

Beside me the girl reads aloud. Her mother leans forward, and the girl speaks without interruption. She places emphasis on certain words, deciding as she reads what's most important. She's creating the story. She is not a gaping mouth, waiting to be fed the fiction of herself.

Her mother drags from a cigarette and exhales blue smoke. Looking into the liquid snow pouring outside, I imagine the mother and daughter elsewhere. The cigarette smoke becomes breath in the halting cold of a Montreal blizzard. The pair huddle together against the side of a building as clouds hurl gusts of snow at them—I must believe it is a difficult place to live—and Carl enters their scene, taking a short cut across Carré St. Louis, where he's going to remember me, our last day together. His neck and chin wrapped in a red plaid scarf. I can see just his eyes. They're watering, but only from the cold.

Water appears in the places I least expect. There are two creeks that run under my parents' house, the one I grew up in, far up the hill above Spanish Banks. My parents bought when the neighbourhood was still economically mixed, when front doors were left unlocked, when fathers came home from work every day, when older women in the neighborhood were visible and accessible.

When my mother left again, I was thirteen and it was winter. My father worked two jobs to pay for the housekeeper he hired. He went to bed at 9:00 each night. I tucked him in to ensure that I would see him,

14

at least a little, every day. Every night he fell asleep with my hands rubbing his feet.

On the Sundays of her absence, we rode the miniature train near the Children's Zoo in Stanley Park. I was too old for it. He did not want to talk about what was missing. We were trying to be happy. This was what she wanted.

Our basement began to flood regularly that year. Some people said the creeks were rising. Beneath that land there was a flux. My body began to emulate the salt content of the sea, primordial, able to create life. I began to bleed that winter, without her. Afloat without devices, without guidance. I straightened the family photographs. I tried to keep the ocean at bay.

But I carried the harbour everywhere, like a life inside me. I wonder if other mothers recede when their daughters become women. Or do they read the paper more intently, not look at their girls so often, refrain from excursions to the swimming pool as soon as their daughters' angular bodies ripen with curves. Is a mother's final distance from her daughter an expression of her disappointment that she too is a woman, just a woman, after all?

Mother says the rise of small buds on my chest did not shock her. The fact that her longest departure coincided with my growth was accidental, she says.

So I looked to billboards for answers. I looked into the expressions of colourful people in magazines. Underneath the glossy photographs, in the negative, in the dark, there is always something else going on, something everyone pretends not to know. I will be a mother in this cafe. Perhaps there will be no father nearby, no one available to disappoint. Possibly Carl will visit. Me and the one inside will not move to Montreal, not even for the winter.

I wonder what I will do tomorrow.

Now the girl skips across the cafe. Life is full in the room around her. She occupies the present. She will not grow up dreaming about women in chiffon dresses, carrying martinis, bored out of their minds, waiting for something.

II

WOMAN WITH A MAN INSIDE

You are a woman with
a man inside watching a woman.
You are your own voyeur.

Margaret Atwood
The Robber Bride

Open Zoo

WHEN SHE TAKES THE SMALL BOTTLE OF lemon juice instead of the family-sized one off the shelf, she suspects she might be leaving him soon. Over the last few months she has been pushing her cart through the aisles, buying small boxes of laundry soap and two-roll packs of toilet paper. She has been thinking David would be on his own soon and wouldn't want the place cluttered with reminders of their sharing.

At home in the apartment she drops her grocery bags on the kitchen floor and leaves them there. The rooms are quiet. Almost everything in them looks mournful, though she enjoys the clutter of old furniture, weary pieces deserted by former tenants of the various places in which she and David have lived since they left high school. In the sunny corner stretches the new sofa David bought with his second paycheque from the firm. Flagrant, creamy leather with sharp edges, gleaming white, and dishonest as a lottery ticket.

She moves through the kitchen again and checks the chore board posted on the fridge. It's her week to shop and unload the groceries. She heaves the bags from off the floor then shoves soup cans and instant noodle dinners into the cupboards. David is supposed to vacuum and do laundry this week. Possibly he will do his chores tonight, which, she decides, would be an unfair time to break it to him.

But she imagines telling him anyway: turn off the Hoover, Honey, I have something I have to say. He would stop vacuuming, put a hand on his hip and smile, *You want your green sweater washed in cold, right? I already did it.* Her sister Valerie's voice enters the daydream: *Don't leave him. He doesn't cheat on you and he washes your clothes for God's sake.* But when she finally says she's leaving him, his face will change into the one she is dreading—his smile drops, and his eyes squint, full of disbelief, as if someone has been run over in front of him.

The eyes on that face are always about to cry, and the lines on his forehead bend into pleading shapes. He says those words, *Please don't go.*

She will have to wait. There can't be any apology or hesitation in her voice this time. She tried six and a half months ago to leave, but David suggested separate rooms as a solution.

"I'm nearly thirty," she said. "I've never lived by myself. I think it's important that I know I can."

"You want to leave a working relationship to be alone and hate it?" David said.

"I've never been with anyone but you," she said.

He said, "Is that what this is all about?" and fanned his arm in the air. "Go on, find out what you're not missing. I won't leave you because of it."

Then she said, "You're my best friend," and started crying. He said, "Exactly, you're mine, too." Then he offered to sleep in the den.

He does not hear the gunfire between them, she thinks. He does not know there's a war on.

She decides to cook dinner anyway. The recipe for *tabouli* calls for one-third of a cup lemon juice, which she pours over soaked bulgar wheat as David comes through the kitchen door wearing his only suit and carrying an Eaton's bag.

His lips taste like banana chips. Once he's finished kissing her, she runs her tongue over her lips and wishes she wanted another kiss. But all she wants is the taste of banana. She sucks the spoon dry of lemon juice.

"My dad's coming by tonight. Feeling kind of lonely. You don't mind, do you?"

"He doesn't like *tabouli*," she says.

"Doesn't matter. He'll eat it. Guess what I bought?" He grins and points at the bag.

"I don't know." She tries to make her voice sound playful.

"What do we need more than anything?" He pulls out a four-slice toaster—brand new with the warranty taped on the box. "No more burnt Sundays."

She says, "Right," and thinks of "Three bucks? It's only worth a dollar"—words he had said ten years ago at the outdoor flea market while bartering for their two-slice toaster, which only browned three sides and usually burnt two of them. She had stood beside him laughing. Her hair was long and thin then, like wisps of fine copper wire. She remembers it batting against David's shoulder as he haggled. The trees around them—their leaves shuddering and falling in drops of gold and red. Down the back of David's pants her hand massaged as far as it could go. He loved the feel of her fingers sliding under his shorts and pressing on the last vertebra of his tailbone. He carried a knapsack then, big enough to hold a toaster, text books, groceries and a sleeping bag. So they stuffed the toaster into his pack and carried it home to their attic suite, fixed tea, made toast and ate in bed the rest of the day.

"Say goodbye to Old Smokey." He unplugs it and places the two-slicer on the floor beside the recyclables bin.

She says, "Don't."

"What?"

She looks down.

"For sentimental reasons?" he asks, smiling.

The thought seems to please him.

"Yeah," she says, but suspects herself of storing the appliance for the day she will move out. She must be ready to meet the words of her sister, "Expensive as hell out there on your own, you know." She will be armed with a response: "I have all the appliances I need, Valerie. I don't need to buy anything."

"And I bought another dress shirt," he says, unwrapping the plastic from the shirt. "Feel it. One-hundred percent cotton."

The pinstripes are mauve-coloured, placid rows on a grayish background. "Nice," she says.

"As soon as I'm called to the bar," he says, "I'll be able to afford another suit, too."

"Right," she says, and then a feeling she hopes is courage swells in her. "David?" she says, trying to remain calm, do normal things like chop parsley into a bowl, blending the green flakes carefully together.

He says, "Can it wait a minute? I've got to deal with a few papers."

She can hear the panic setting in. He knows. He does this every time, finds a distraction—a cheque book that needs balancing or a curtain rod that's in sudden need of some glue. One time he suggested they go for a drink. "Mom and Dad never went out when they were still together." And when she agreed to the drink, thinking they would discuss their impending separation over a glass of beer, he insisted on sitting at a table with a built-in video game. He slammed quarters into slots, pounded buttons and laughed sheepishly at himself, "I just want to have one more round."

"David, I need to talk."

"About what?" His face moves into that expression she can't stand even imagining, the one that says, Do anything, but don't leave.

Possibly it is not really his face that she dreads. Sometimes the face more horrible is one from a street corner long ago.

She was fourteen at the time and ready to run, aching for a chance at life outside of town, of her neighbourhood, of her house. Dreams full of limitless space, weeds and vines, of morning glory, foxtails and dandelions growing wherever they pleased. She would have room in this place to stretch and run free.

Her father took her to Davie Street for a lesson. "You run away, and that's the face you'll look at all your life. Filthy old buggers with no morals, thousands of them. You want to kiss those types? That's what happens to the girls who run. Look over there—you think she's glamorous? She's just a goddamn whore."

She kept her eyes on the man. She watched him touch the breasts of the girl whose hips rubbed against the side of his car. His face was thin and full of reproach. He hated her.

23

"I'm showing you this 'cause I care. You've gotta wait for the marrying kind to take you away."

"About what?" David repeats.

"Nothing," she says, "it can wait." She turned instead to the lemon juice and calculated how much of the 225 ml bottle she had used. Two more bowls of *tabouli* and the bottle would be finished.

She lies on the bed, eating. The sound of David's feet shuffling in the kitchen and the scraping noises of her fork on the plate hang static in the bedroom, hers. They had become house-mates this year, except for the occasional kiss and tribute to their sexual past.

The silence in her bedroom makes her feel as if her throat is clogged. There must be a place to shout. Another house, another city. She doesn't know where. She looks at the phone. The rest of the world is on the other end of it. She picks the phone book up, scans the first pages for long-distance directory assistance and area codes. Anywhere. Dials 1-212-555-1212. The operator says, "Good Evening, New York Telephone," but she doesn't know anyone there and hangs up.

She visualizes herself jumping in the car, driving across the prairies, not knowing where she is headed. Mary Tyler Moore driving to the Twin Cities in her early-seventies hatchback, and then that music: *You might just make it after all.*

What if she doesn't make it after all? What if she can't find a job, or a proper apartment? She will have to live on the street.

Her fingers dial 1-514-555-1212 to hear: "Bonjour. Bell Canada, what city please?" in a heavy French accent. She likes the sound of it. She says, "Pardon me?" and lets the operator repeat herself. Then she hangs ups.

The phone rings as soon as she puts the receiver down. Her sister's voice is raspy from too many cigarettes, excited because of a job offer in Whitehorse, and full of long sentences about how she will be moving there next month and what she will take. After a long silence Valerie says, "Well?"

"I just can't seem to tell him."

"You're just going to have to leave, I guess," Valerie says. "Though you know how I feel about the whole thing."

What you need to see is a bruise, she wants to say. The problem here is that I have nothing to show you. I can't give you a quick-sentence explanation:

He had an affair.

He comes home drunk every night.

He deals cocaine and puts our lives in jeopardy.

All that he's done since we got married is go to bed with two women, but he didn't have intercourse with them, so that doesn't count, right? He comes home drunk once a week, which isn't much I guess. Most of his friends deal hash to supplement their incomes. Why should that concern me?

"Can I come with you?"

"I don't think you'd like it," Valerie says. "Neither would David. There's a lot of darkness in the winter. Dad doesn't think I should go, of course."

"I meant just me, by myself."

"I guess," Valerie says. "But you should think very carefully before leaving David."

"Have I ever told you that he tells me to 'fuck off, bitch,' when I try to wake him up off the sofa?"

"What?" Valerie says.

She repeats herself.

"It's hard to believe."

"It's sort of easy to forget, too. He doesn't even remember doing it. The next morning he gets up early and makes *huevos rancheros* or some other exotic dish for me. Brings breakfast on a tray with a yellow rose in a vase, like something out of a movie."

But she doesn't believe the breakfast tray is for her. It's for his mother, and he is his father, and she and David are stand-ins, rewriting the wrongs. She has known this always. He's deeply in love—with an idea: a lasting marriage, one that doesn't end in a courtroom, bitter with children split from their father, the father so lonely.

David comes into her room, smiles, and points at the plate and fork on the floor. "Can I take that?" There's a dish cloth over his shoulder.

She nods, says "Got to go" into the receiver, waits for Valerie to say goodbye, and puts the phone down.

"Mind if I sit down here?" he asks, looking at her bed. "How was work today?"

She says, "Go ahead, sit. It was okay."

The bed hardly moves as he kneels on it.

Years before, it would move like a sea and they'd pretend to be stranded, taking waves across their water bed, rolling from edge to edge. They stripped thin shirts off each other's backs. His long mane of thick black hair. His lips smooth across her shoulders.

Take off that suit. She wants to say this, but not because

she desires his body naked. Take off that suit, and quit reminding me of who I'm not, of how many decisions I haven't made.

"You need a break," he says while his fingers etch their way down her ankle sock. "That's what you want to talk about, isn't it?"

She pulls up her sock. "Yes. I just want to go." The more room you give, she wants to say, the less room there is that's actually mine. The movement I have is *given* to me, doled out—an open zoo, an illusion of liberty.

"We could take a trip. There's always that trip to Asia we wanted to do. Or you could apply to a professional program, say. What's another student loan at this point?"

"David, I've got to go for a while," she says, competing for his attention with the door bell ringing.

"That's what I'm saying. I agree."

"I don't know for how long."

"As long as you come back," he says, laughing. "Duty calls. Got to get the door."

Once he has left the room, she constructs a scenario: her boss in the morning, how she will quit, the letter she will write David, explaining herself perfectly. The clothes and books and trinket things she will miraculously fit into the car. The room in the shared house she will find. Or, rather, the basement suite without windows she will have no choice but to rent. What if she actually had to sleep in a park? What if she could not make it after all? She foresees the panhandling she'll do, the street walking, cold nights. Her scenario collapses into the sound of her father's voice rising: *I told you so.*

"Hell of a time parking around here," her father-in-law says from the kitchen.

"Hi, Randall." She flashes a smile at him from the bedroom door.

With her shoes in hand, she rushes into the kitchen. David is scooping *tabouli* onto three luncheon plates. "I thought we could have toast, too," he says.

"I can't stay, David," she says.

Randall looks at the floor.

"Off for a little drive." She smiles apologetically at David. "I'll leave you two to do some talking."

"Well, have fun," David says.

Randall says, "You modern couples."

"I guess," she says.

David scrapes the *tabouli* off her plate and onto their two plates, building mounds of it.

She watches them not looking at each other for a moment. "Maybe I'll take some of that with me," she says, grabbing a container, heaping some into it.

She opens the fridge, not wanting anything in particular. A sack of Red Delicious stares out at her from the crisper. She takes the whole bag and then stuffs a block of cheddar into her pocket. She watches her hands claw at containers as if the hands are appendages on loan, stashing food for the winter ahead.

David and his father are quiet. She glances at Randall, catches his look of concern. If she runs now, David won't start hunting her down until Randall has left. Maybe she can get away this time for good. Maybe she won't return a few days later, tail between her legs. She feels David's look on her, but she can't meet his eyes—they'll be flashing a red warning. A stop sign. Danger ahead. For your own safety, stay inside the compound. Do not leap the fence.

She finally looks up and brushes with the face she has been expecting. The eyes. The forehead, bunched in the shape she knew it would assume. His mouth—about to speak, but silent. Her hands keep on moving. They close the fridge and turn the knob on the front door.

"Hey," David says. "Where's all that food going?"

"Visiting," she says.

He says, "I was going to make Dad an apple crisp for dessert." He forces a broad, easy smile and puts his hand on Randall's shoulder.

"Oh, I see," she says, walking back to the counter. "Here." She lifts apples out of the sack. Then she moves quickly to the door, not wanting a look from either of them. Taking the knob in hand again, she tries to find the momentum and conviction she had only a minute ago.

"That's not enough," David says. "It'll be a pretty flat crisp."

"I don't mind," Randall says. "Let the lady go do her visiting."

"Have all of them," she says. From out of her bag she pulls the apple sack and leaves it against the wall.

"What else do you think you're taking?"

Randall stands and fusses with the lining of his coat pockets.

"You've left me cinnamon and brown sugar, haven't you?" David continues. "You're not taking staples."

"I think I'll use the washroom," Randall says.

"No, Dad," David says.

"Stay, Randall," she says and watches her hand lunge for the front door, which she opens, and then closes from the other side, the outside.

She had always planned to take the grand flight of stairs easily—with long, confident steps—but her sense of stride is waning. Maybe tomorrow would be a better day to leave. Her legs keep moving—they persist in taking her down the stairs, closer to the landing, and out the apartment building.

There is no time to pause, even. She is in her car, starting the engine, not waiting for the right moment or a sense of direction. She accelerates into a line of traffic, thinking only of freeways.

BROCHURE TO SAVE THE MARRIAGE

THE DAY BEFORE THE FIRST DAY: FLIGHT CX800: Nap over Japan. D. wakes. The twins in *Twins* separate. Buffooning actors drag each other across lines. I hold D.'s hand because I am trying. We glide over the dateline. Today comes after tomorrow. Yesterday will catch up soon. Everything rides on this, the vacation of miracles. Laughter. On the plane we use it like medicine. We pour it over Eroica Hair Tonic for Men, the vomit depository, & the plastic bags telling us to Arrive in Better Shape. When we land we get an extra day & a shoe horn. Things look possible.

Day One: Peanut butter bun with a piece of insect. One glass coconut milk. One beer. HiC orange drink.

Day Two: Filet o'fish. Small fries. Trucks tow baskets of skinned animals, waiting to be hung in street vendors' stalls. Carts take narrow streets, teeming with socks, fruit, Panther brand underwear, shelled walnuts, live chickens. D.'s underwear needs replacing. Elastic shot.

Day Three: Ride a sampan steered by a young girl through the junk boats in the typhoon shelter in Causeway Bay, Hong

Kong. D. snaps a photo as we leave. I tell him he is culturally impenetrable. He says I should be more impenetrable. I remind him that we agreed not to mention C.

Day Four: The store across from our hotel is called Golden Marriage Co. All You Need. Bed linen. Sheets. Napkins. D. says when we get back to Canada we should have a separation agreement made. He announces this after our fight in Chatter Park. We are supposed to put C. behind us, that is my position. I am a liar, that is D.'s position. Around us, middle-aged women do Tai Chi exercises. I want to be one of them. I do not know anything about them. C. would remind me of this. He is coming up, a lot.

Day Five: We take the subway to Wong Tai Sin, a city in The New Territories. Once we arrive I smoke a Marlboro & fall asleep for an hour, dreaming of C. He boards a plane. A flight attendant holds his hand across the Pacific. In my dream he is prone to trembling. Not sure what he is doing.

Day Six: We land for a two-day stopover in Bangkok. A gang of pre-schoolers play tag along the six-lane highway we're riding on. I start to think about babies. I don't tell D. because I know it will upset him. For dinner we eat car exhaust with the meat on skewers we buy from street vendors.

Day Seven: All day people sweep the streets & the sidewalks. Still, dirt everywhere. We visit three Wats & a giant golden buddha, reclining. At one of the temple grounds we enter a massage tent made of fine white cloth. Rows of white beds: white bodies caught in the act, receiving back rubs, leg rubs. We pay. We take our places. I can not look at D., the sensation of four hands moving along his legs. I turn to face the billowing walls of the tent. Fingers press into my scalp. Later, a stoned blonde man serves us *Gado Gado* for dinner & collapses on the restaurant floor.

The brochure to save the marriage said, *You Save $600.00 By Adding A Stop In Koi Samui, Thailand, Before June 2nd.*

Day Eight: D. lies on his back, head entirely submerged in Thai waters & hears cracking, like glass. There is a sound between his ears. His brain is splintering. Ear wax, I say. Two couples dance on the beach. All are topless. Beyond the couples there is nothing, an empty beach.

Day Nine: Sand like brown sugar. Sand between D.'s fingers moves inward, fisting. At the beach-front massage tent, a woman named Mama feels up a girl who strips off her shirt. Mama says, "You've got one titty bigger than the other." The girl drops her cotton pants & climbs on the massage bed. The masseuse scans for witnesses.

Day Ten: Lightning flashes against noisy palm trees and falling coconuts in the wind. Dark sky hangs over a bathwater sea, flashing yellow for an instant. Clouds rumble, anxious. Rain spills from the air like a colourless drape, unrolling continuously. D. wants to go to the disco across the island. Out of the sand, I sculpt a man's face & shoulders. He washes away in the tide. I write a postcard home: *Thailand is not a cure. Exactly. Wish you were here.*

A bulldozer arrives to remove palm trees. Mama points the driver toward the trees surrounding the restaurant where we are sitting. One of our dining companions looks terrified except when she laughs, loudly. Her boyfriend drinks something called a Blow Job. He tells a chirping bird to fuck off. Finishes the last of his burger, throws a piece of burger lettuce onto her plate. D. says the guy's haircut reminds him of C. I want to be in Thailand, along with my body. I watch two wild dogs & three pigs play cat and mouse on the sand.

Day Eleven: Sun stroke. Scaly bumps in patches on both our arms & thighs. I'm stuck at 39.4 degrees. Diarrhea in the squatting basin. Mosquito larvae breed in the water container. Slime covers the gritty floor. D. & I lie under mosquito netting & watch bugs fall through the holes. Take turns staggering to the restaurant for pots of ginger tea. Don't think either of us has felt this generous for months. D. reads to me from a travel brochure about the Bulak Laut Bungalows in Pangandaran, Indonesia.

Day Twelve: Sleep.

Day Thirteen: We move into the brochure's life.
In a strategic position right by the beach freely face Indian ocean and white sand. Far away crowd and high way pollution. Greenish circumstance with fresh oceanic air. Bungalows in bamboo house and unique interior design performs peaceful joyment. Advantageous

location in the west coast near Animal Preservation, so the evening can be seen, the sunset, the flying bats. With family and relatives the right place for spending holyday.

Children in gangs put their hands out at us & say, "Hello, Mister, give me money." Then they laugh. I decide to spend the rest of our downpayment savings. We dine separately on Tuesday. Later that night we make love for the first time in a month.

Day Fourteen: A woman in a bamboo cap & rubber thongs walks onto the motel compound & stands before me with a sack of fruit over her shoulder, saying, "500 rp. for a pineapple. I'll chop it up for you." The rp. translate into a couple of dimes. I am already eating a pineapple, though, & she can see this. I shake my head, but she remains, until I look away for her to leave. She walks back one kilometre to the marketplace in the midday sun. I know it is a kilometre because I went there this morning. My chest wet with sweat, and nothing but a camera over my shoulder. I feel watched by C.

Day Fifteen: D. & I play in the waves. Something is keeping us together. We move into the sea & don't know it. I look toward the shore & cannot find it. Waves rise on all sides of our bodies. I can no longer see D. A wave presses violently on my head & drags me out. I am nothing. My will is flat. D. is visible in the spaces between bursts of wave. He is fifty feet east. The water jerks me under & out, further from him. Under & out. I think, This will be a quick death. Once I understand this, the fear is gone. This death will be peaceful. But my body thrashes. I rise above & watch my body try to save itself. It is calling, "Help me." It swallows more water. It holds its breath. Its arms are enormous suddenly, doing the front crawl & not moving. Everything that is known, the shape of D.'s face, is precious. D. is the only person the body wants to say goodbye to. It wants to mouth, I am sorry. D. yells to the body & gestures: GO SIDEWAYS. DO THE CRAWL SIDEWAYS. NINETY DEGREES TO THE SHORE. When I understand the body will live, I return to it. I am crawling up the sand, people watching. I go on. The journey is exhausting.

Day Sixteen & Seventeen: We do not leave the motel room. We lie on the batiked bedspread, staring at the bamboo mats on the ceiling. Bodies ache to the touch. The strain of the fight, immense strength of water. My shoulders burn as if every muscle & ligament has been torn.

Day Eighteen: We sit on the concrete outside our room & watch the waves that nearly took us. At lunch, two men approach & ask about the children we don't have. "Hello, Mister." (I am not addressed.) "Where is your country? Are you married? Is this your wife?" They try to sell us chocolate buns & a knife with an intricately carved handle for only five dollars. "Come on, Mister. Good knife. Sharp." I think we should buy it. I nod approval at D. He says, "I really love you sometimes."

Day Nineteen: D. goes to the Monkey Forest without me. I stay alone at the motel. Like every other tourist, I cannot understand anything. How can I see anything in this place? *I hear your voice, even here. Hope your studies are going well. Happy*

Birthday. Can't decide whether to send this card to C. It takes me two hours to write these sentences. Sending it would be a sign of weakness. Not sending it would be a sign of weakness. I mail it.

Day Twenty: Jakarta: Concrete with fierce traffic. That is what I can see. We take a taxi to the airport, an Indonesian pop tune sung in English hums from the front dash: "True love means planning a life for two. You fill my dreams. You are my life forever." I laugh wildly. I go over the top. D. is solemn, just like our driver. I have offended them both.

Day Twenty-one: Singapore. One-night stopover. We take a tour bus to the famous Open Zoo, an animal reserve without cages. I pose for D.'s camera, holding a mother chimpanzee on my lap. She is shaking. Of course she wants to get off.

Day Twenty-two: CX801: We fly home holding hands. I throw out the postcards in my purse. In my shirt pocket I carry loose tea picked from plantation fields across from the motel compound. We will drink it until there is no more.

In Hiding

I AM WATCHING HOW SHE DOESN'T WATCH ME. Instead, she looks to the ground, not trusting it, and stomps. All her weight switches onto one leg, and she stands, unmoving—it's some kind of test.

"This is a bog," she says, taking her glasses off, staring at the earth beneath us.

"Only in parts," I say. "Come on, let's walk."

"This isn't going to take very long is it?"

I say, "Mom," and wish my voice didn't sound hurt. She looks at me quietly. "All right then," she says and fixes her glasses back over her eyes.

We move through the forest together. She keeps a step ahead of me, watching the ground mainly, careful to stay on the path of cedar chips. We graze the branches reaching at us. A slash of fiery autumn, tangerine and gold-red, claws up the hill in the distance, and I say, "Isn't that beautiful?"

She glances up and stares for a moment. "You know, I haven't seen a patch of moss like that for a long time, Colleen. It's lovely."

I look into her eyes for as long as she lets me and wonder if we'll ever see the same things. "I meant the trees over there," I say, pointing, and my mother says, "Oh." And then,

"Have we done enough now?"

I tell her I thought she loved walking. That's what I remember her doing when I was a little kid, during the years that she wasn't away. But I don't say that.

I'm expected to forget her absences, and recall one of her many nights spent at home, frying bangers and boiling cabbage, the steam rising around her face. She said these were Dad's favourite dishes from England and that my sister and I, being his children, should have loved them too.

But as soon as we dragged crusts of bread across our plates, soaking up the last slick of sausage drippings, the dishes went into the basin for soaking, and my mother took to the back door—with a flashlight in the winter. She left us for an hour or more and walked a circuit around the neighbourhood.

"I do like walking," she says. "On streets."

"I just thought you'd like a break from sitting in that dingy hospital with Baba."

Her pace quickens and she is not as careful about the path. "I don't know why you've started to call her that. You were taught to call her Grandma all your life and now you think..."

"All her other grandchildren call her that except me and Valerie."

She says, "'Baba'—it sounds like a noise a sheep might make."

I say, "It's your language."

She turns, laughing, and I'm not sure if she's laughing at me or at wings flapping in the tree beside us, the fuss of branches, the confusion among starlings. I keep walking and say nothing.

I didn't say much in the hospital either. I just watched my

mother talk to her mother. With one foot firm on the floor and the other tucked under her thigh, my mother leaned against the edge of the hospital bed. She spoke consoling words in loud and slow English to my grandmother's worries, whispered in Ukrainian. "No, you haven't ruined her party. We'll just postpone it till next week when you're better."

I made sounds like I was clearing my throat.

"Over here," I said. My mother turned. I took a few steps toward her and my grandmother, aware of their faces side by side. I always hope to see what I don't see—a shared expression, the same eyes, or a common gesture—branches of the same thing.

"You shouldn't sneak up on people like that," my mother said.

I said, "It's only me."

My grandmother's hand, tough and thick with veins, reached at me. "Collie," she said. Her big knuckles and callouses squeezed my hands, which looked so unused next to hers.

I said, "Hi, Baba."

My mother turned and looked out the window.

"Happy birthday." My grandmother pointed to her bedside table. "For you, your present." She kept pointing.

I opened the drawer and took out a parcel wrapped in red and black scotty dogs. "Thank you. You shouldn't have troubled yourself, Baba."

"Uh-huh," she said, nodding and smiling. "Trouble is no, not trouble."

We stayed another few minutes, long enough for my mother to explain what the doctors had said, that Baba was to stay in the hospital for two days under observation. No, heart palpitations didn't mean she would necessarily have a heart attack.

My mother stops beside a tree that looks like it's had an axe taken to it. She touches the sinewy yellow flesh—a slash of the fibrous bark hangs like twisted rope from the point where the blade met the tree. Deep green firs, so dark they're almost blue, lean over us, while thin waxy branches of young maple—no taller than ourselves—wind into each other. My mother is looking, and I want to know what she sees.

"Let's talk about something else," she says.

I say nothing.

"So this is your favourite trail, is it?" she says.

I nod and she asks why.

Because of things that do and don't happen here—all fun and no danger—but I can't tell her about coming here with gangs of kids and lying in piles of leaves all night with arms around a million souls, and how we all looked to the moon, and I saw my mother in it, convinced she was protecting me in this dark forest. I can't tell her about walking down the trail to Spanish Banks, sitting on the sand till dawn, waiting at the beach loop to catch a bus home. I always arrived home, it seemed, just after she came off her sleeping pills. She was most relaxed with me at those times.

I walked across the room to her side of the bed. With slurred words—she was still under the murk of the drugs—she asked, "Is that you, Colleen?" Her eyes were calm and her face loose, not yet tensed for the day. Her hand reached slowly for her glasses, and only in this moment could I steal some unguarded bit of her. "What are you doing up so early?" she asked.

"I couldn't sleep," I said.

"Lord, don't be like me."

"Quit putting yourself down," I said, and lightly touched her leg, through layers of thick Hudson's Bay blankets. "Let me get you some tea," I said, and when she nodded, I leapt off her bed and almost ran into the kitchen, thrilled to get away with making her tea. Ordinarily she wouldn't let me, preferring to show how well she could do everything on her own.

I walked back into her room, precise and steady while placing her best cup—garish roses with gold leaf around the rim—on her bedside table. She was gone then, face awake, eyes sharp, leaning toward the window, fingers nervous and batting at her falling hair. "Thank you," she said. I imagined she was trying to smile. I sat on the bed again.

"It's Saturday today. I guess you have lots of homework." I said I did. "Well, you'd better get to it if you want to make something of your life, dear."

Sometimes she would go away for weeks, which Father would call a "rest period," and I'd come into this forest and read all afternoon, then walk home and wonder what made my mother so tired and if I was the one who was wearing her out.

She had been taking these rest periods ever since I was born, or so it was implied by my aunts, who hushed family secrets over their tea cups. Their phrases came in drips, abrupt and pellet-like. "Not suited to motherhood. Snooty. Too good for her people. Mishandled by doctors. Never needed them in the first place." And on and on. I said, "Someone should tell me what the hell's going on." But no one ever did. My mother was as delicate as heirloom china, and no one wanted to risk breaking her by revealing to me the details of her problem.

"I have good memories here. I love the way the branches arch." And I love how rested my mother looks under the fingers of pine and fir, interlocking over our heads, making a safe roof. I want to tell her this, but instead I say, "I like the smell."

"Funny, I was just thinking about this smell. There was a dump site near the church where I grew up and men used to burn garden refuse there. Leaving choir practice in the fall— this was the smell."

There is a soft bluish mist breathing all around us which I've only just realized is smoke, coming from up ahead, almost in gusts. Burning leaves smell different today. My mother inhales with her whole body, eyes closed.

"As a teenager in the Ukrainian..." She opens her eyes. "...in the girls' choir...I sang there until I married your father in his church, you know."

"I wish I could have belonged to something like that. A Ukrainian group."

"Not this again."

"Well, two of my grandparents..."

"You have no idea what it really meant."

"No, I don't."

"It meant being on the bottom of the pile when I was growing up. It meant my father being paid less by the greengrocer he worked for than the Englishman who did the same job."

My mother's voice is stale, monotone; the words must feel old and tasteless in her mouth. "It meant being so poor I shared a bed with three of my sisters till I was twenty-three years old. It meant an orange and a few nuts for Christmas. It meant being taunted in school. I wanted to change my name to Stevens or Hughes. It was not like today. Or maybe it was."

I don't know what to say to her. She is not loosening—she's not giving me a place to come in.

"I just do my best to forget about it," she says.

The smoke is getting closer and thicker and I ask if it's burning day, but my mother says it isn't.

I can see wet marks moving up the sides of her shoes. She stomps through marshy bits of decaying leaves, making her feet even more damp. The path is no longer soft. Tree roots gnarl under our shoes. It seems that one of us should trip.

"I wonder if mother's going to make it," she says.

"The doctors seem convinced she will," I say.

"She's eighty, Colleen." And then, "Say, why don't you open the present she gave you?"

"I'd rather wait till my birthday."

"Mother never lost her pride," she says to the ground. "Well, when she did, it was never about being Ukrainian. Come on, let's see what the present is."

I know what it is because I went shopping with Baba last week and told her how I wished we spoke the same language and that I would try to learn hers soon. She said, "Your mother," and I'm not sure if she meant, 'You can learn from her,' or 'If you want to talk and shop, go with your mother,' which was impossible since my mother never went shopping with me, and the few times that I pleaded her into it, it became some awkward routine of mimicking what I'd seen my friends do downtown with their mothers.

"Please," she says, and I hear how odd the word sounds coming out of her mouth when it's directed at me. I take the parcel out of my purse, rip a corner of paper and pull out the book. "Oh," she says, "I see." She fingers *Ukrainian—A Guide for Beginners* lightly, hardly touching it. "Well, that's nice."

There's something missing ahead. I can see, or rather cannot see, what should be there, what has always been there and now isn't. I'm not believing my eyes, how far they can see without a single tree to block the horizon. I look at the sign beside me. Salish Trail. Yes, this is the right path, but it has ended too early. What was dense and green, and twenty acres of it, is now scattered in piles of ash and cinder, still smoking—signals into the sky. An assembly of Cats lull on a heap of mulched trees: the Christmas-tree tops of evergreens, flattened under tons of equipment.

My mother says, "You dropped this," and hands me the book, not looking at me. I hear myself say, "Oh," and my head is full of something thick and condensed.

"This was important to you."

I say, "It was... my trail."

She turns to me, stern eyes, but watery. I wonder for whom or what she is crying. I don't ask. I just take her by the arm for as long as she'll let me. We stumble over charcoal logs, through shadows cast by trees on the perimeter. My mother is unsteady and slips over a patch of black mud. I lose her arm, but she stands, regains her balance. Her hands move into her pockets, arms tight against her body.

Miss Sixteenth

ACROSS THE STREET LENA IS DRESSED IN BLACK linen, creased and lumpy. Her face has folded into itself so that her nose and lips look smaller against her fallen cheeks. She waves at Joy, making her gesture big and warm. Joy steps off the curb toward Lena and then stands beside her, noticing only how poorly she has aged. Joy apologizes for her own stopped watch, which hasn't really stopped, and for being inordinately late, though she never meant to be on time. She had planned to slip into Lena's house, slide through the maze of black suits and dresses—without snagging herself on a memory—and to say "I'm sorry, Lena," but not as a condolence.

But Lena does not seem interested in Joy's story about her watch. She gazes at the man walking across the street toward them. He's wearing a long black coat and scratching his scalp. Lena says to Joy, "That's Garret, my boyfriend," and looks to the frosted blades of grass beneath her feet. After a pause, she says, "He came to the funeral with me. So did Colleen. She's waiting in the house for you."

"I'm sure she came to see you," Joy says.

"I never said she didn't," Lena says.

Garret arrives beside Lena and says, "Don't look so down—at least they left you the house."

Lena nods.

Garret's pragmatic thinking doesn't appear to offend her. Lena has always tolerated too much, Joy thinks.

Joy hoped this would have changed. She had hoped—earlier in the day, while preparing for the memorial—that Lena would be handing out hard slaps across the face, or, at the very least, eloquent brush-offs to all her parents' former accomplices-in-silence who would be attending the memorial service.

Some people, once they've grown, pretend to have forgotten their persecutors, even when facing them. Others wear scars like fresh cuts. She didn't know how Lena would be. Joy explained these things to her nine-year-old daughter, who stood on the bed watching Joy paint a red line around her lips.

"I have to go," Joy said. "The invitation said 'Please come.'"

"You don't really have to, Mom."

"I do," Joy said. "I was bad to her. So was Colleen."

"How bad?" Allyson said. "Tell me something you did."

Joy paused, not wanting to admit to details. "Allyson, I'm telling you because I want you to know that people do change. Do you understand? Even the girls in your class."

"What did you do, Mom?"

She looked quickly into the mirror and saw the new shape of her mouth, pursed—a container of words that might spill like prized coins for Allyson to use indiscriminately—and pulled the lip-brush along the centre, zipping herself shut. "Never mind," she said.

◆

Lena hopes she can produce a line of sweat around Joy's

hairline. She wants Joy honest.

She puts her gloved hand on Joy's shoulder. "They spoke of you often. 'What ever happened to Joy?' Dad would always ask. 'Skinny little Joy.'"

"I wish you'd forgotten all that," Joy says.

"Why?" Lena asks, but Joy starts chattering about the time that has passed, and oh, what a pretty neighbourhood this still is. The sky is more interesting, so Lena watches it—the mauve light of dusk settling over Joy, Garret, herself. She listens to the limbs on the bare winter trees stretch in the wind and arch against the sky. She is almost gone, off to Athens or New York, some place, severely polluted, that produces a swath of sunset, a purple haze every night. Suddenly, Garret tosses his arm over her shoulder, and she returns to where she is standing. His lips press into her face. He does not touch her lips. He says to Joy, "See you inside."

Joy barely skips a beat in her talking. "Oh, right, of course," she says, smiling at them, just a little nervously. "See you then."

Lena does not know how to tell him she doesn't like his approach.

◆

For a moment Joy watches Lena squirm between Garret's arm and body, then she walks back across the street to Lena's house. She curses her cowardice. "Oh, right, of course," she says aloud, mimicking her own compliance. "Rape her if you must." She can't stand how much she needs to be liked these days, how much she is willing to compromise for a smile.

In front of Lena's house, now, Joy watches Lena kiss the man's neck and look up at him slowly for his approving eye. Her look is the one Joy has been dreaming of lately, the look of childhood—the face, the pleading face Lena gave her brothers, her father, her mother, before one of them could find an excuse to strike.

Joy could never figure out in advance how Lena would be punished for her accidents and mistakes. The punishments seemed entirely arbitrary. Some days Lena's tripping down the stairs would only earn laughter from her family. Another day, one of her brothers might tell her to come to the top of the stairs, and then kick her down again, reprimanding her clumsiness as she fell. Once Lena forgot to add onions to the sauce she was cooking for her mother, and Joy was witness to the result. Lena whispered, "Claws, claws," during the beating, and her mother shook and shook her, yelling, "What you saying?"

"Nothing," Lena said softly, looking up at her mother with that pleading face.

"Say nothing," her mother said, and stopped shaking her. "That's right. You say nothing."

But Joy had heard Lena clearly. She had heard it before.

She stands on the doorstep of what is now Lena's house, the house of their common childhood, the House of Horrors—as she often called it. She wonders if the house was left to Lena, and not to her brothers, as a final act of torture. Even in her parents' deaths Lena might not find freedom. Lena will be burdened with a house full of ghosts.

Joy taps on the front door and lets herself in. The hallway smells as always—of almond candies, olive oil, dust. She's relieved to find that she recognizes almost no one. Strangers in black. Two women weep together on a sofa covered in clear plastic. Metaxa and Ouzo and sherry bottles are everywhere. A group of old men toss worry beads between their fingers. Two

49

young men trade stories about the brutality of car accidents. They stand over trays of cookies and honey-lemon cake, the sight of which makes Joy nauseous.

When she enters the kitchen, she sees the old man's prized dinner chair. She can imagine him sitting in it, speaking gruffly. He tells ten-year-old Lena she can't go out until she's finished the meal on her plate.

"But I can't finish it."

"Look at your friend Joy. Look at her. She's thin and she finished hers."

Joy beamed her pride at the floor, pretending modesty.

"But you gave her half as much."

"You're fat. You need more."

The smells are overwhelming. But Joy must wait, she tells herself, for Lena to come into the house. She must wait so she can take Lena into a corner and whisper that children abuse their power with each other, that she did not understand what she was doing twenty years ago, that Lena must move away from this house, this block, and make a second chance for herself.

A finger nudges Joy's ribs from behind. She turns, dreading all the possibilities.

"Thanks for coming," Mike says.

"Mike," she repeats his name, not knowing what to say after that. 'Good to see you'? But it is not good. She says "Mike" again, and nods her head.

"Lena appreciates your coming," he says. "I know Mom and Dad would have been glad."

"Yes," Joy says. "Well, thank you."

The brother with authority, still speaking for his sister. She used to take the end of his belt on her face and never breath a word about it. Does he still think about doing such things? Does he remember the power his parents gave him, the sounds he forced out of Lena's mouth? The panic of the neighbourhood children, the solidarity of their terror. Lena's cries piercing the composed neighbourhood air. Joy's own mother covering her ears. Her father saying, 'It's family business, we can't interfere.' Mike had accomplices in silence too, and Joy is one of them right now, still, because she is nodding pleasantries instead of saying, You are the meanest fucking bastard I ever knew.

♦

Lena lets Garret hold her hand because she wants to appear happy and in love as they walk into the room. Garret guides her toward Mike, who says, "Hey, it's The Fang." Mike turns away from Joy, mid-sentence. Lena watches her old friend smile politely and excuse herself to the bathroom. She knows an escape when she sees one.

The men have stopped talking, and Lena can feel Mike speak to her although he's saying nothing. He wants a drink. He wants her to make it. The message is all in his glass, the way he is dangling it toward her.

She can feel her nails suddenly growing, knuckles bending. She has known the feeling since childhood: the way her hands, at any required moment, can transform into paws. Her breakable nails become claws, as sharp and strong as sickles, poised for attack.

♦

As Joy moves to close the door to the bathroom, she catches a glimpse of Colleen, then continues to lock the door behind her. The small white tiles covering the walls and floor give the room a cell block quality. In front of the mirror she breathes deeply and examines her skin under the unfair fluorescent light. She is older than she thought. Lines conspire around her eyes and mouth. She has left things too late, too many years have passed for her apology to affect the truth of anything.

She resolves to leave, and then she notices the metal weigh scale.

She can see herself again, stocking feet stepping on the scale, the gauge reading 76 pounds and Lena's mother saying, "That's beautiful." Then Lena's wide bare feet steeping onto the scale lightly, quietly, as if gentle movements might reduce the reading. And Lena's mother slapping her head. "It's because you're a pig. One day you're going to break my scale."

When Joy leaves the bathroom, her eyes land on Colleen. "She looks like she's having a gay old time," Colleen says. Lena licks the bottom of a shooter glass. "Who's that vampire she's with?" Colleen continues. "He's got erect coat lapels."

"No idea. Some guy called Garret."

"Someone Mike hauled out of the sewer, no doubt," Colleen mutters. "Christ," she says, quietly between her smiling lips. "She caught us staring."

"Keeping an eye on us is one of her survival instincts," Joy says.

"Don't start dredging that up," Colleen says.

◆

Lena watches Joy and Colleen in the spaces between the family friends and old women who came to mourn in sturdy black outfits and brogue-like shoes. The shoes remind her of her father, but no tears come when she thinks of him. No, as soon as she conjures him up—there, on the living room floor, a guest at his own memorial—she sends him back. She holds the reins now. She does not even need her claws.

But the two wiry friends across the room will not leave. Although she had invited both of them, she expected no more than sweet lip service from Joy and Colleen—hello, are you keeping well, do call if you need anything—and that soon afterward they each would vanish. Last week when she was addressing invitations to the memorial, she was struck with the urge to have her childhood all around her. She wanted these friends to witness her success, to see how she had overcome the odds. But their avoidance of her, their deliberate politeness, makes her feel she had overcome nothing.

Watching them stand there in their slim-fitting clothes, in their stylish bodies, Lena remembers them in their gym shorts, t-shirts and runners.

It was an afternoon in late October. The slim girls had decided to remake Lena in their own image. They ordered her into gym shorts like theirs, a t-shirt, and runners. If she didn't do as they instructed, if she couldn't run the circuit around the block in five minutes, they would make her do an additional lap. They stood on opposite corners with watches in their hands, reminding her at every lap that she had agreed to this beautification of her body.

Her claws nudging out of her fingertips. Each crack in the cement was a bone in one of their bodies. She said, *I tear out your femur* and lashed out across the crack, or *This is your skull* then clawed the crack. She jogged with her claws fully extended. Joy and Colleen kept her out till 7 p.m., watching her pant along the sidewalk, thighs red and rubbing, into the damp night. She collapsed and threw up at Colleen's feet.

Jack Andrews, the neighbourhood watchdog, came out of his house and said, "I've been watching you little bitches." He picked Lena up, wrapped her in his coat, and carried her home.

◆

"I was in the shrine," Colleen says, "and you'll never believe what I found."

"A ghost."

"Guess again."

"I can't," says Joy. "Why don't you forget about snooping around here and come visit Allyson instead. She'd love to see you."

"Tomorrow, I will. But listen, I found the crown."

"You're dredging," Joy said. This was her warning bell. She and Colleen shared a common past, each remembering certain incidents the other declined to.

"No," Colleen said. "There's nothing here to dredge. It's on the surface of everything."

Joy feels her head lighten as Colleen leads her into the little room that was once a shrine. When they were girls, the room was made of yellow light, cast by small round candles floating in oil. Gilt pictures of the Virgin and saints, wearing golden auras and bluish gowns, covered the walls. Every day Lena lit a candle and said a prayer for her dead grandmother. Every day she checked that the candle was still burning. If she did not, her mother sent her to her brother's room, and he could decide what to do about it.

In place of the particularly large saint who once commanded the room, a bookcase now stands. The edge of a paper and foil crown hangs over the top row of books. That the crown still exists is a surprise. That Lena has it is more of one, since she had never been Miss Sixteenth Avenue.

Joy can hear Lena laughing and she's glad for it. It is testimony that everything did turn out all right after all, that no permanent damage was done. Lena giggles in the hallway and says, "Don't do that." A moment later Lena laughs so hard that it sounds like she's choking. Joy peers out of the little room. Garret is standing over Lena, breathing down her neck, saying, "Be a good girl." He holds a snifter to her lips. "Do as I say." Lena pulls out of his grip and glances at Joy.

"Right," Lena says.

Joy returns to the little room where Colleen tops her own head with the crown.

Colleen says, "Why did we fight to wear this thing?"

"We should have let her win, even once," Joy says. Colleen says, "She was so damned persistent."

Every year Lena entered the contest, performed her talent show—a line of cartwheels, which, Colleen announced, made the ground shake. Along with the other competing neighbourhood girls, Lena paraded along the boulevard, showing her legs, tossing her hair over her shoulders, sticking her chest out.

Every year she did not win. When Joy and Colleen were the judges, they could be certain Lena would not rank among the finalists. In the years they were contestants themselves, Joy and Colleen influenced the judges with promises.

One year neither Joy nor Colleen won and they turned to Lena, not for comfort, but *as* comfort, a pillow, a soft thing that couldn't punch back. In the hierarchy of hurting she occupied the lowest rung.

◆

Lena waves at Garret through the front window until his

car is out of sight. He has left her for a six-pack of off-sales. She has twenty minutes. She walks across the house toward the old holy room, lowering her head.

Colleen sits on the bed with the Miss Sixteenth crown tilted on her head, taking swigs from a Metaxa bottle. Family liquor. Who the hell was she anyhow? Joy pulls the crown off Colleen's head as Lena enters the room.

"I just keep that thing around to remind me of the good old days," Lena tells them, without irony. She leaves the room with pride, perfectly, snootily, in a manner just like theirs.

She hopes they are feeling burdened with guilt.

She hopes that for the next eighteen minutes she does not dwell. There were some good moments to be had from the contest. Lena had the opportunity to be proud, the proudest she had ever been in front of other girls. She had marched up to the judges table and announced how her mother had spent all morning baking a honey-lemon cake for the contestants. She listed every ingredient in the cake, how the egg whites and yolks had needed to be separated. Her mother had lost two eggs in the separation process and did not get angry. Her mother was as good as other mothers. This proved it.

But before the shiny crown could be placed on the winner's head, Joy announced that the winner, who was new to the block, had plain brown hair that could use some gold streaks. Lemon and honey are yellow. "It'll make you blonde," Joy said as she and Colleen smeared Lena's cake into the hair of the queen, who ran home crying that year. Lena stuffed the biggest crumbs into her coat pocket and walked home, proud that she had been spared, that they had not smeared the cake into her hair.

In her room later that day, she crawled under her bed

toward her skinny victims. She clawed the carpet, scratches and scratches to add to the perfect bloodless markings already there.

◆

"She'll get us back one day," Colleen says.

Joy fingers the crown and says, "Allyson came home with gum in her hair last week," not looking at Colleen. "She said she rolled onto it in the gym."

"Well maybe she did," Colleen says.

"She's wetting her bed again—at nine years of age. And someone cut a hole in the back of her shirt yesterday, so she asked me to start picking her up after school."

"Kids are bastards."

"We should have let her win, even once," Joy said.

With a bottle of Metaxa hanging between her fingers, Lena comes to the doorway again, smiling. "It's good to see the two of you together again."

"Excuse me," Colleen says and leaves the room.

Joy feels a tightening in her throat. The thought of Allyson being so faithful to the girls in the gym, of her being doggish, fond of her oppressors, forces Joy to grind words out between her teeth. "How can it be good?"

◆

Lena really wishes Colleen hadn't left. She sits in front of Joy and asks, "Why did she go?"

Joy looks at the floor. "She feels badly, you know, about the past, I think."

"No, no," Lena says. "It's good for me to see you both. You two are familiar. You treated me like family."

"Please, don't say that."

"Remember that time I had a cold and you and Colleen came and sat with me all day rubbing Vic's Vapo-Rub on my chest."

"Jesus, Lena, we made you eat it."

"You didn't know better. I know you didn't." She looks to the wall where the huge saint used to be, and holds the Metaxa bottle against her abdomen. "I'll have to buy candles and keep this room for them. In memory. Like Mom did for her mom." She hears a lack of balance in her voice, a shakiness. She cannot believe she is doing it here.

She can feel them, the wet lines on her face must now be obvious to Joy. "I'm still going to miss them, even though." She leans against the bookcase and holds the wood siding like something to love. She slides onto the floor for some measure of control.

Mike comes into the room and she knows she's done for. He acknowledges Joy by purposefully keeping his back turned to her. He crouches and looks sternly into Lena. "Keep it down, girl."

"Right, Mike. Sorry." She feels the sharpness breaking through.

"You must keep it down."

"Fuck you, Mike," Joy says.

Mike's face is blank. His mouth is a cold line drawn across his narrow ugly face.

Lena feels Joy's delicate hand on her shoulder.

The claws are coming on more strongly now. They are long and powerful and could flick an eye out in one swipe. She looks at Mike and then Joy, deciding between them who shall be first.

In Place of You

AN INK PAD SITS ON HER FATHER'S QUEEN ANNE desk. Anne-Therese rolls the date stamp carefully, exacting the correct year, month, and day. When she's certain all the numbers are aligned, she grinds the stamp into the pad and slams the date onto a sheet of writing paper in a quick one-two motion.

She writes:

Dear Colleen & Keegan,

But crosses out baby Keegan's name. Better that than include the father's. She puts the pen down and thinks of what she can possibly say.

Across the room, a blue box sits under the china cabinet. It has been waiting for three weeks. The City Engineering Department delivered the box along with a pamphlet detailing instructions on dividing plastics, stacking newsprint, washing cans and removing their labels and lids. The instructions don't indicate how to remove the gummy labels from glass jars, only that it should be done.

She is afraid of the box. Colleen would not understand this. Unlikely, unmarried Colleen—now tucked at home in a little cottage on a Gulf Island, nesting with her baby and some man,

apparently Danish and completely unknown to the family—
would scowl at her resistance to the box.

Colleen still tries on princess's shoes, then a pauper's pair,
flitting in and out of political groups, flavours of the month,
degree programs, universities, derelict cars, four different ad-
dresses in one year, always between jobs, and now between
scant men, men's beds. She does not really know this, but she
can well imagine.

Poor Colleen. Her father never really disciplined her.

Anne-Therese opens Colleen's last letter and looks at the
photograph. Colleen looks worn. Frayed bits of hair frame her
face.

*How are you? Getting enough sleep? How is the baby? The
photograph you sent was lovely. You and the baby look very healthy.*

The photograph shows the three of them. The man looks
very much like Colleen's ex-husband, David. David had given
some stability to Colleen's life. Of course she abandoned all
that.

Anne-Therese can't decide what more to say. Beautiful
things are always being destroyed these days. She puts her pen
down and takes in the scene across the street. Children she
doesn't recognize pick weeds from the Craiggs' unmowed lawn.
It would have upset Anne-Therese's mother, God rest her soul,
to behold such a scene. She had never before seen a home
deserted on this street. The grass is brown with thirst and
almost as tall as the children, who have begun to lash each other
with the weeds.

Twenty years ago, Colleen might have been one of them.
More often, Anne-Therese remembers Colleen playing in the

bathroom, stooped over the enamel sink filled with water.

She first liked to play in the backyard for hours, harvesting the dill, raspberries, cucumbers and Sweet William with her sweet grandmother, Anne-Therese's mother.

"I am a Bedouin," Colleen said. "I haven't had water for thirty days. Have you a ladle?"

Colleen's eyes were glassy, her mouth hung open like a stray dog's on a dead-hot summer's night. "Water," she said. "I will use my hands. Come. Share with me."

By scooping her hands in the water, she drank the basin dry and became Colleen Mainwaring again, aged 12, daughter of Alex and Eva Mainwaring, wearing blue-jean pedal-pushers, North Star runners, and speaking like the A-student she was. "Things taste good only when you haven't had them for a long time. I believe in self-deprivation."

Deprivation. She could not know how much she sounded like her grandfather. He was dead by the time Colleen was born and no one ever talked about him.

I am keeping quite well. The weather is very warm, but I don't suntan anymore. The sun is much harsher now than when your mother and I were girls.

Your mother should have told you so many things, Anne-Therese would like to say. If your mother had raised you with authority and guidance you would know where you belong now. If your father had taken full control of the situation... But she can't say this—it's better to be quiet about these things.

Quiet, peace and quiet—that was Eva's style. Quiet. Quiet. That's all Anne-Therese ever heard coming out her sister's mouth. Especially before she ran out of their family home, quietly, through the basement window late one night, and ever-so-quietly married Alex Mainwaring, 23, a young conservative, dreaming of political life, dedicated to the sport of rugby—and always somehow flaunting his smell.

He was a gentle man, though, and often gave Anne-Therese bear hugs, whispering, "You'll be all right, Anne-Therese." She never knew what to say. What on God's earth are you talking about? But she didn't ask; she took the hugs and remembered each one.

Eva Mainwaring quietly announced her marriage by letter, once she was three thousand miles away. Never again would Eva stand in the kitchen doorway, saying, "You can't keep this up, Father. We need peace. This must stop." She was the only one of his children to stand up to him and the only one to cry in front of him, pleading for kindness.

And their mother would be on the floor, her forearm up in defence, her head down, eyes down, crying, never loudly. She promised in Ukrainian and English to make a better stew.

Eva had her way of staying out of control and clear of her father. She was the only one in the family to leave the neighbourhood. She spent her late teens learning how to drive a car. She went to dances. She took hour-long baths. She went through jobs like a child eating vegetables, taking a bite here and there, throwing it all away at the slightest bitterness or distaste.

While Anne-Therese worked ten years for the same garment manufacturer, Eva had eight different bosses. She had no staying power and neither would her daughter. Then again, it is impossible to predict these things. Anne-Therese could never have guessed at the unlikely outcome of even her own sister's life.

Do you remember the Craiggs? You used to play with their eldest child, Diane, when you came to visit. Audrey Craigg died last month, not even a year after her husband passed on. Even in death they didn't part.

Audrey Craigg, how veiny her legs were. The Craiggs lived for three generations in that house, invested pride in the garden, the produce, their children. Nothing was left to run wild. But now the kids are either dead or living in different cities across the country. She and Audrey spent many hours on the porch front, stretching in the sun, toes pointed, turning at all angles, flexing their calf muscles at each other. How they compared everything. They touched hands and pressed their fingers together. Anne-Therese's fingers never reached the smooth, long tips of Audrey Craigg's. Sometimes they would keep holding hands, minutes after the comparison was over. Audrey always looked as though she never noticed, as if holding hands was an everyday thing. Anne-Therese feigned casualness, too, trying to make herself unaware of their clasp. They'd soon get onto the subject of children and before Anne-Therese knew it, she was holding her own hand across her chest.

Although Anne-Therese never had children of her own, Colleen was her surrogate child. During most summer vacations, Eva and Alex flew in with their girls for a visit. Valerie was never much interested in being coddled, but Colleen seemed to love the extra attention only an aunty could give. Colleen was so bright, so much more everything than the Craigg girls.

Remember how little Diane Craigg married her husband because she was pregnant? Remember she left him just after the baby was born? I just received word that after four years of separation, she's gone back to him. I'm so happy for them.

She looks more closely at Colleen's photograph. She has always thought Colleen was one gene away from beautiful, that she had the kind of face that could be exquisite or completely hideous with the slightest genetic change. Colleen had always been between extremes. But Anne-Therese has never known which way she would swing. She has only hoped.

Colleen writes that the man is an excellent father to the baby and that she's never been happier. She asks, 'Why don't you write anymore? Is it because of my divorce?' Anne-Therese doesn't know what to say to this. She puts the letter back in its envelope and tries not to think about it. Clearly Colleen no longer believes in the self-deprivation she enjoyed as a twelve-year-old over the sink. She must live with the faucets completely open now.

Keegan's a very bald baby. How did that happen? You had a lovely head of hair at birth.

But then she crosses that out. The man's genes must be responsible.

Diane sent a photo of her young family. Her boy has very little hair just like Keegan.

She crosses out those sentences as well—they are a complete lie.

Across the street the children of Mr. and Mrs. North get out of a new car. They've moved back home to live with their parents, but not in the way Anne-Therese lived with her mother. These children live at home to be supported by their parents, not to support them.

The North children are the same age she was when her father called together all six of his children to announce that he had decided Anne-Therese should be the one to tend and manage Mother after he was gone. Anne-Therese would take Mother to church on Sundays. She was the best-disciplined, he said. She was the one least afraid of duty. For her effort, she would inherit the house. It was unlikely she would marry, he said, since she was twenty-nine already and no one had yet asked for her hand.

She reminded him then of her other plans, her business ideas. A woman's function, he said, is to serve her husband, and if there is no husband, then she is to obey the father. He suggested she talk to Father McKay about her predicament. The Father said she was free to choose between right and wrong, between obedience and selfishness.

I prefer bald babies actually. It makes them seem younger, and so people tend to dote upon them for a little while longer. Babies do love attention.

What she'd like to say to Colleen, in answer to her question, is the truth: no more dreaming. The truth is that Anne-Therese has stopped dreaming *for* Colleen. She no longer imagines possibilities for such a girl. The Theatre, some had predicted: Colleen would land in the centre of the greatest stages in the country. She would become Canada's version of a Broadway queen. How thirsty she could make herself look. How earnest she could be with a bath towel wrapped around her twelve-year-old head, speaking with an Arabic accent.

Colleen was no different from the rest. She would not bring the family special recognition. *People* magazine would not pound at the door.

Now Colleen had reached that age when one becomes just like the rest of the relations after all: investing in all the wrong risks; succumbing to the lure of new furniture and dinner parties with the latest china in her cabinet. How the world stops asking about a woman's future once she has arrived at one.

Anne-Therese imagines how it happened for her mother, how she had arrived in Canada sixty years ago and landed a future that offered few choices: married young, pregnant a month later, her belly routinely large with babies and worry.

After Anne-Therese's father had been dead a year, her mother took off her black dress and wore floral prints until she died. Anne-Therese did not protest. She was glad to be done with the ghostly figure that hovered around the stove, wordless, stuffing cabbage leaves or boiling oats. Anne-Therese welcomed a brighter future for the two of them—with florals, and parties, even. But after a day spent watching each other shuffling around the house in slippers, neither Anne-Therese nor her mother had energy enough for an evening with guests. The house remained colourful, but still.

Are you in contact with David at all? Easy divorces stop people from working out the rough spots.

She stares at these lines for a long time because she knows they will make Colleen angry. Anne-Therese figures she could teach even the most resistant person a thing or two about duty. She could be a scholar on the subject.

When she was twenty-nine, she wanted two weeks off work to take her ladies' suits to the fashion forum in Montreal. Women in the neighbourhood had been buying her designs for years and they all anticipated her fame, even bragging a little when they were the first to buy from her new spring line. Anne-Therese worked hard at fitting each neighbour properly. She often took the bust, waist and hip measurements two or three times, just to make sure she'd sew the perfect fit. How perfectly a woman's curves could complement the embraceable texture of a soft rich wool.

She asked for two weeks off, and her boss offered her more. "Take a whole lifetime," he said. She went to the forum with suitcases full of suits and returned home, her bags as heavy as when she left. The lines and the lengths were all wrong, she was told. The materials were second-rate.

She took a job as a teller and learned to enforce the rule of numbers behind a bevelled-glass partition. Juggling dates and debits and credits was easy work compared to the challenge of carving garments from cloth. But more respectable, her father said.

Your grandparents marriage wasn't built on a bed of roses, but they stayed together for nearly forty years, you know. Your grandmother had a hard life, but she knew the full love of one man.

And the hate. But such ugliness is not worth retelling, Anne-Therese thinks. Love, love is what's to be remembered. It was love that made him so protective. He always stood in the doorway of the living room when she or Eva had a visitor. Anne-Therese and Eva played cards on the coffee table and talked politely to the boys, eating Mother's poppy-seed cookies, while Father leaned against the door frame, watching. Then slowly, and without much resistance, his eyes would close. When the alarm he had set earlier in the evening rang, he expected the boys to be gone, and if they weren't, he told them to put their coats on and get the hell out the door.

Eva said they were "abused children" long before Anne-Therese had ever heard the term. But by that point Eva's mind was probably scorched by the pills she had been taking: the anti-depressants and God knew what else. Her versions of events were questionable, weren't they? Anne-Therese never asks her sister the exact reason for her current drug use.

Eva has carried pills in her purse since Colleen's birth.

The recovery was never quite complete, as far as she could tell. Nonetheless Anne-Therese has made it a policy to remain cheerful in letters, especially in ones to Eva, especially on the issue of family.

Anne-Therese prefers to say that their father used a strong hand. He did beat them afterwards, but those were the rules: No boys after 9 p.m. He always hit Eva the hardest, and she always managed to remain somehow disrespectful, no matter how sore she was. He only got to hit Anne-Therese once for breaching the 9 o'clock rule, and wasn't much interested in the beating. He said it was because she reminded him too much of Mother already, dutiful, hands clasped, praying in a corner. And anyway, having a girlfriend over past 9 o'clock was not the same thing.

When their father died Eva sent a condolence card to their mother, but she didn't come home for the funeral.

Are you getting enough sleep, Colleen? Really? Just try not do too many things and get your rest. Babies are hard work. You've done so much in your life already, just like your mother. Slow down.

Which reminds her of the announcement Dr. Alan Thompson made during her last visit: "You, Anne-Therese, are the oldest virgin I've ever examined. Congratulations." Anne-Therese thought she might find pride in this fact, but she has told no one. If she were to tell Colleen, she knows Colleen would laugh and probably tell the man, and the two of them would sit with the baby in their bed and say, What a deprived old bat. And maybe they would be right.

And maybe they would be wrong. Maybe they would be struck down by God, or the ceiling might strangely cave in on them as they were laughing together in their unholy bed. Where is her real husband? Where is the man to whom she is truly responsible?

She can feel herself starting to sweat at the thought, her heart beating out of her chest. She wants to lock the door, not let anything in, no more wrongness. She wants to run across the street and find Audrey Craigg alive and say, Audrey, come run with me under the open sun, through a summer field. Come touch my hand with your face.

She holds onto the desk with both hands.

Do what you can and no more. If you don't get a meal on the table one evening, it's not the end of the world. Don't waste your time trying to be exceptional now.

Across the room there is that damned box. She hopes Colleen isn't wasting her moments alone with this kind of rethinking. Trying to reverse the world's problems, like Colleen might, is like telling the sun it must start to rise in the west, she thinks. She keeps trying to think. Her heart is still going. She decides to put the box to better use as a container for her gardening tools. Knowing your own earth, knowing your place and reaping goodness from it—this is the most valuable thing a person can do. These days, however, her knuckles bother her when she tries to plant or dig. And the earth, it seems, is fighting her. Soil is not soft and compliant in her hands. It does not want her touch.

The box still sits there. Everything around her is lashing back, or dying, or not giving thanks, or leaving her with unwanted furniture, with a great-nephew in an ungodly union, a depressed sister, women in the newspaper doing whatever they damned well please with the world and each other and not listening to the order.

She will not burden Colleen with the details. It is her responsibility to be cheerful.

Take care of yourself and Keegan.

Love, Aunty Anne-Therese

Anne-Therese starts to address the envelope. Colleen signs her letters from the three of them, but they all have different surnames. The baby's is an anagram, of all things, a rearrangement of letters from Colleen's and the man's surnames. She does not recognize any of them.

BELONGINGS

AVID DID NOT NOTICE HIS OLD CAR PULL UP. He continued to heave boxes marked CAREFUL and OF SENTIMENTAL VALUE from the truck while talking absently with a man whose name he could never remember. He only found it necessary to converse with the man every couple of years, and only when moving furniture for his ex-wife's best friend.

"So, David. I hear you're living in the City Hall area."

"Nearby, I guess," David said. Although the man wasn't entirely accurate about the district, David and his fiancee *had* recently moved.

"Well, congratulations on your son," the man said, lifting GRANNY'S CHINA. "He's beautiful. We've got the picture you sent on our mantle."

David did not have a son and for a moment he didn't understand why the man thought he did. "You must be talking about Colleen. *She* has a kid now."

She had failed twice at leaving him, but finally succeeded the day David was called to the Bar.

On a clear afternoon in the late fall David had received the news regarding his employment future. Carrying his job offer in hand, he had left the office in a celebratory mood, walked

71

smack into the cool air (still earning an articling student's wage, without money for a winter coat), jumped a bus, got off at the Government Liquor Store, bought a bottle of Mumms and a newspaper announcing the fall of the Berlin Wall. He stuck his thumb into traffic, knowing it would be the last time he would hitchhike, having become, in one short day, legitimate: employed with prospects of a bank balance. He was no longer bound to a fierce little budget that relied heavily on Visa cash advances.

He walked home with brisk strides. He approached the gate to his apartment and noticed Colleen standing outside the door, holding her stomach. He raised the brown bag into the air and cheered, "I made it," forcibly ignoring, he knew, her nervous stomach, not wanting her to unload another doubt.

He moved closer, kissed her hard on the lips. He wanted to say, Don't wreck this for me, but, by saying nothing, she already had.

Before they could enjoy the bottle together, she packed up and left for good.

The man quickly passed David a box of shoes and boots. By the look of embarrassed sympathy, David knew the man was now recollecting the bits of gossip he had heard, piecing together the story of David's separation. The details of his life had undoubtedly circulated around the coffee tables of many people he barely knew.

"God, sorry," he said. "I just can't keep up."

David said, "Neither can I." He held the box. "I can carry more," he said.

The man passed him PHOTO ALBUMS: PRECIOUS.

◆

Colleen got out of the car, slammed shut the rusted door and balanced on her shoulder four pizza boxes and a thin package wrapped in Santa heads. She approached the moving truck with confidence, nodded at the man, then at David whom she hadn't seen in two months.

The sky was as cloudless as the day she had left him crying in the doorway of their apartment. The grass and the dying geraniums in planters were the same brown as a year ago. Even the evergreens seemed to conspire to remind her.

"I got your favourite, David," she said, huddling the boxes under her coat, rushing into the house, breathless by the time she reached the top of the stairs. She stood on the landing, chewed a hangnail momentarily, and wished she could give up her old habit of buying for David's tastes.

She had recently read an article entitled "Finishing Him," in which a therapist said it takes two years to 'complete' a failed relationship. It had only been one year since she had walked out.

She moved into the kitchen, avoiding appliances laying on their backs, electrical cords extending everywhere, half-hung curtains. While stepping over a tea pot on the floor, she tripped and sent the pot careening to the wall, smashingly, but it did not break.

The pizza boxes dropped to the floor. She shoved them into the oven and went looking for Joy. Peering into the dining room, she tried to block from her view the room she had once called *The Joy of Sex* den. She and David, as teenagers, had performed The Book, page by page, contorting their bodies into every illustrated position.

Colleen found her further down the hall, stretching on a thin beam of winter light that moved across the mattress in Joy's parents' bedroom. Except for the loud sunlight that glared from every window, the house was quiet. Joy's great hair fanned out above her head, wispy twine-coloured strands spreading madly over the bed of large blue roses. Joy's mother had vacated the entire house that day for a rented apartment which would give Joy and her two kids, and her husband—if he were to come back, and she were to let him—a clean house in a secure neighbourhood, rent free.

"I'm going to change the wallpaper in here," Joy said, smiling at the freshly washed carpet, at the garbage bags marked UNDERTHINGS. "And the drapes," she added.

"You look well," Colleen said, carefully. "Really."

Joy smiled wider.

The smile was closed-lipped and knowing, and it protected Joy from questions she might not want to answer. It was the smile she had used during the many afternoons they had been together as Husband and Wife. Colleen had always played the Husband, trying to remove Joy's nightie, first caressing her shoulders, then kissing her neck, and Joy was the Wife, giving her mother's satisfied closed-lipped smile, quick to squirm and roll over, saying, "Not tonight, honey."

"Remember how we'd swing from those drapes playing Jungle?" Joy said. She brushed her finger along the fringe of the drapes, then crunched a handful of the heavy floral material into a ball and buried her nose in it. "I love the smell of old dust."

"Don't you want to talk about it?" Colleen asked.

"No," Joy said. She tipped over a hefty bag and poured

74

white bras, lacy silks and flannel nighties onto the mattress. She sorted them with great concentration. Garish blue roses climbed all over the bed.

Colleen wanted to grab her and say she would have no trouble meeting someone else, but Joy started to sing. She wanted the subject changed.

"Husband and Wife" or "The Affair"—Joy said she could hardly remember either. But Colleen thought vividly of their kisses regularly. Joy played an obliging Mistress, taking off her nightie, wrapping her legs around Colleen, saying, "Darling, take me." But Joy really preferred to play the Husband coming home from work, unlocking his front door, walking in the house to find his Wife (Colleen) in bed, her hair tousled, and accuse her of wrongdoing. Joy loved to howl, "How could you do this to me?"

Affairs had shaped both their marriages. Joy had discovered her own husband Quaid on top of their babysitter last month. And David was in the kitchen now avoiding her, no longer her husband, because of the many games that had been played. She had low expectations of Husband and Wife, and a desire for The Affair, with its promise of passionate legs and nighties on the floor.

If Colleen hadn't become proficient, as a ten-year-old, at scripting love scenes, would she have approached Carl two years ago with the expectation of a similar kind of excitement? Would she have talked to him after class, explaining how much more interesting he was than the instructor? Would she have invited him to the student pub, confessed her marital problems, found his blue eyes so deep, his compassion overwhelming?

Would she and Carl have a child today had she not played The Affair? Was her life entirely arbitrary?

David came into the room as soon as she thought of him. A slice of pizza in one hand, a string of white cheese hanging from his beard.

"Thanks for the prosciuto," he said. His long back stretched cold and thin in the doorway. She thought of him naked suddenly, how his shoulder blades jutted out so harshly.

She said, "Wait," and handed David the package wrapped in Santa heads. "Here. Merry Christmas."

He made no move to take it. It was the first Christmas they had spent apart in eleven years.

"Can't I still give you a gift?"

"I have nowhere to put it," David said.

The gift was a piece of cardboard cut into the shape of a cat. The manufacturer's packaging read 'FLAT CAT—The Ideal Low Maintenance Pet.' Colleen had not meant to buy it. She had only been walking Robson Street last week for the effect the sidewalk had on her baby. The sloped curbs and broken pavement lulled him to sleep, so she pushed him in the buggy up and down the length of a block where the Flat Cat had stared out at her from a shop window. The accompanying words drew her into the store.

There are two kinds of women, David had often quipped, high and low maintenance. He had always said Colleen was the former. She asked why he didn't leave her then, and David always said that wasn't his point.

◆

David took the package under his arm. "Tara's coming to pick me up. I can put it in her car." He looked at Colleen standing there and felt himself smile. She no longer lived with him. Never again would he have to listen to her schemes—her plans to take exotic vacations on credit, borrowed time and money. How she thrived on complete uncertainty.

She often said she'd rather die than know how she was going to spend the next week.

◆

Colleen said, "Right, there you go, Tara's car will do," and returned him to another time. Off went the beard, glasses and Rockports and on went the frayed jeans, Dayton boots and a mop of ratty black hair.

He had smoked himself brainless in his late teens, the late '70s, introduced Colleen (a girl from a cloistered neighbour-hood—there was a Catholic Nunnery on the corner of her street) to a subtle variety of hangovers, and given her the ability to identify pot plants from regular house plants at a glance. She and David spent many evenings together in anyone's basement, carousing with friends, most of whom had since ended up in jail, or completely reformed themselves into churchgoing family people. After such an evening, Colleen and David would drive to the beach, take a blanket to the sand and dream their future together. He vigorously, she hesitantly. He had decided on the year they would buy a house, the month they would have their first child, the kind of modest vacation they should take.

She'd asked, "What would you do if I died tomorrow?"

"I'd be sad for a long time," David said. He puffed on a

cigarette with great solemnity. "But I'd meet someone else and get married. But don't worry, you won't die."

When he spoke this way she wanted to kill him. He was too certain of their common fate. She did not want a bit part in her own life. If she wasn't there to fill the role he'd scripted, a faceless Colleen-substitute was ready to advance at any moment. Colleen knew Tara was allergic to cats. She was not the perfect substitute. Unlike Colleen, Tara could not fill a bowl with Salmon Delight, empty a litter box, hold a cat on her lap, or even share the same air with one. Tara had an especially violent reaction to the short-haired cat David had bought near the end of his relationship with Colleen in an attempt to fill the gap, the space growing between them. The cat was their child, their trial run at having a baby.

The tabby Gigi had a double-barrelled surname, her own dishes, her own bedding, and medical appointments. Colleen and David took her for her shots together, nervous first-time parents, their eyes filling.

◆

"I'm going to get another slice," David said. "Good deal you've got here, Joy. Your parents are amazing." He left the room shaking his head. Colleen looked malnourished and green, he thought. He had heard her say something about breastfeeding sapping all her energy and how she still got up five times a night. He had never seen her baby. He could not imagine it, him.

He walked into the kitchen and took the last slice of pizza from the last box.

◆

Colleen looked at the green plastic bags in mounds

throughout the terribly square room.

Joy said, "This is my bedroom now. I'm going to be sleeping over the spot where I was conceived. A little too close to home, isn't it?"

Colleen said, "Where are the hangers?"

"But then again," Joy said, "how could I afford to turn down Mom's offer? Free rent, a chance to save for a down payment. I have to admit it's nice finally to be safe like my mother was, safe from choices." Joy stood in front of the mirror and wrapped her hair into a puffy, loose bun—a flattish bouffant.

"Even when I was a kid and that insurance agent was hanging around, wanting to take Mom away for the weekend to Reno, she said she didn't have a choice. She was married, simple as that." Like David, Joy too had recently become someone else. Having two small children and an absent husband helped speed her metamorphosis. Her days were no longer new, and there were no beginnings anymore, only extensions. She was finally the age she had always wanted to be. Ten years earlier, Colleen had dragged her into night clubs and discotheques, engaging in perfunctory rituals of what she thought it meant to be twenty. But she knew Joy had really been waiting her whole life to be thirty, and looked to forty as a place of comfort, warm memories, a savings account, toting arm chairs to the beach, sitting in the shade, and not being obliged by youth and vigour to lie on gritty sand under the full hot sun.

Colleen suspected Joy would always wear a nightgown to bed now. Her attention turned to David eating ravenously in the kitchen. She watched him take more than his share of garlic toast with his pizza. The other men leaned against shiny appliances and drank beer from cans.

Before she could imagine something about David, pretend to know about his new life, the trouble he may be in, the overeating he could be doing, she heard the men's voices soften as a clip-clip of heels rose in their direction.

◆

David watched his fiancee walk across the hardwood floor toward him. She strode in the low-heeled pumps he had bought her. The shoes had, for a decorative reason, metal taps on the heels and toes that effectively announced her arrival. Her long strides and proud head were lawyerly, he thought, and befitted her new position as a Prosecutor for the Crown.

He was glad for her tactical approach: Bowl them over with confidence. For Tara to appear in the same house as Colleen and Joy, a plan had been required. David had told Tara everything. About the teen sex den in the house, how he and Colleen had been in love for at least half of their relationship, how two weeks before she walked out they bought *What Shall We Name the Baby* at a garage sale and pretended they were expecting. He was always honest.

"My wife left me and six weeks later met another man, who impregnated her almost immediately." He said it on their first date.

Tara, too, had been left.

◆

"What's she doing here?" Joy asked Colleen.

Joy had never expected Tara to arrive. She had never anticipated Tara's or Carl's existence. When she walked down the aisle behind Colleen, carrying the train, she had thought marriage would preserve the couple in a kind of stillness. That the marriage vows would seal the future air-tight, less likely to spoil.

Vows should be preserved. She had said this to her husband last month, but by then he had already broken his word. She had to preserve what was left, and carry each wanted, salvage-able piece of that life into the new house, this new life alone with her kids. Continuity had to remain.

"She's picking up David," Colleen said. "That's why she's here."

Joy watched Tara, the way her tar-black hair framed her face, accentuating her high cheeks, thick red lips and blem-ishes. She wore no cover-up. She looked like someone's first choice, not second.

Tara latched her finger through David's belt loop and laughed. "Some old guy across the street wouldn't let me park in front of his house," Tara said. "He said it was his spot. I told him curbs were municipal property. He said I had better move on."

"Old Andrews got her," Colleen laughed.

"He sweeps the sidewalk every day, you know," Joy said. "He's parked there for thirty years."

"What an old fool," Colleen said.

Joy said, "Maybe not." In her teens she had called him an intrusive old grunt. She did not know what to call him today.

◆

David stopped laughing before he wanted to. He wanted to engage with his wife-to-be, to hold her proudly, to say, I am glad for all that has happened, that Colleen finally did leave me so that Tara could come into my life. He wanted to announce these things to everyone. But then Carl arrived.

Carl and the damned baby appeared in the doorway before

he had a chance. The baby, of course, supplanted Tara as the highlight of the room. The baby kicked and gurgled and waved his arms and the moving men reacted:

"What a live wire."

"Those backpacks saved me and my wife."

"Big boy, that's for sure."

The baby sat in the pack innocently, smiling toothless at everyone—especially David, it seemed.

He said, "Friendly creature," and put the last crust of toast into his mouth. He felt Tara let go of his belt loop and say she just remembered something in the car. He asked her to take the package wrapped in Santa heads.

She walked away as briskly as she had arrived. As soon as David heard her shoes clipping down the stairs, he felt Carl lean toward him.

"So," Carl said. "I hear you're going to tie the knot a little tighter this time."

Joy started to clap and her eyes brightened. She looked past Carl, directly behind him and laughed. "This old man, he played one, he played nic-nac on my thumb," she sang to the baby. She hummed what she couldn't seem to remember.

David knew a great deal about Carl, and he hoped this might work to his advantage one day. He knew that Carl was a penniless student who didn't believe in marriage or in other ways of silencing women's histories. He knew Carl insisted his son have Colleen's surname. He knew Carl had a fear of traditions.

"Well, at least I'm not afraid to tie one," David said, finally.

The last time he had spoken with Carl was at the signing of his divorce papers.

Joy said, "This old man he played three, he played nic-nac on my knee."

At the time of the divorce, David had been articling downtown in a prestigious office, panelled in aged oak, and opulent with its select view of the city's harbour. In an uncharacteristic moment, he had offered his legal services to Colleen, making himself the Husband, the defendant's lawyer, and the respondent's lawyer, all at once.

He endured an hour of watching his wife and her lover grin over his legalese: *Since the celebration of the marriage, the Respondent has committed adultery with Carl Richard Eyre on various and divers occasions...*

"You're right," Carl said, relieving his baby son of his winter wrappings. "I am afraid of the law in my bedroom."

Colleen walked into the kitchen before David could think up a response. Joy's singing ploughed into his thoughts, and he pushed the Old Man, now playing nic-nac in heaven, away.

He watched Colleen take Carl and the baby between her arms. He watched Carl struggle to remove the baby's hat.

Once the hat was off, he stared at the baby's flesh and skull, and eyes like hers. The child was not a phantom after all, appearing only in photographs and phone conversations.

If it were his child, would the eyes be that shape? Would Colleen's genes have been dominant? Might their baby have had teeth by now and be drooling all over Colleen's hand? Would she be teaching the child to say Dada?

He had an excuse to leave the kitchen. The other men had

moved to the living room, and he did not want to be separated from them.

◆

From across the kitchen, Joy yelled, "Hey, Carl, how about helping me clean this freezer out while Colleen feeds the little one?" She did not want him to follow David into the living room. She wanted to keep her eye on him. Left on his own, he might get the opportunity to take the house apart, or deconstruct it. He reminded her of the insurance man who used to come calling for her mother. This man, too, wouldn't leave well enough alone.

If she were to let him into her living room, he could critique the books in her boxes. Would he say that her life was fraught with the wrong kind of literature and weak ideas? She preferred not to know.

Colleen carried her baby into the unpacked dining area and negotiated her way among the boxes, bags of cushions, stacked chairs and table legs with their feet splayed into the air. She sat in privacy among the teetering boxes and manipulated her nipple into the baby's mouth. She became absorbed by the splitting of her selves, these people together, their various demands, the different eras of her life, now merging into something she didn't understand. She felt fragmented but whole, like a completed puzzle.

She watched Tara return to David's side in the living room, with a sleek leather jacket and bolero across her arm.

Tara raised her voice at Colleen. "We have a carpet in our place that used to be yours. We're going to throw it out unless you want it."

"We mean, could you use it?" David said. "Could you come by our place and get it?"

Before Colleen could answer, Carl came out of the kitchen and announced they definitely could use such an item.

Their apartment, however, was fully carpeted.

♦

"I thought you'd want to see his apartment, his apartment with *her*," Carl explained as they stood at David and Tara's front door. Carl held a soother in the baby's mouth. Colleen put her fist to the door.

"Let's get it over with," she said, and dropped her hand against the door, until Tara answered.

Tara's earrings: a table on one lobe, a chair on the other. Colleen didn't need to see the rest of the place. She imagined a solid domesticity of sturdy furniture and functional artwork. But when she stepped into the hallway, she saw herself all over the apartment—her handwriting on spice jars, the pewter mug she gave David on his twenty-first birthday, the lamp they had received as a wedding present eight years ago, now wearing a new shade.

"We've got a party to get ready for," Tara said. "I've got to do my hair if you..."—her voice trailed into the bathroom.

David said, "The carpet doesn't fit where we'd planned to use it."

"I'm sure we'll find a spot for it," Colleen said, suddenly aware of her excruciatingly cheerful voice, of the Saturdays she had wasted buying carpets, of all her planning for a home that would never be. Her and David's attempt at drawing a family tree, pulling lines together from each of their parents to themselves, imagining lines extending into someone not yet born, someone who never would be.

Carl and her dozing baby moved around the apartment together. How would she explain this world to her son?

Photographs stood erect and forceful on the mantlepiece—David and Tara with grandparents, the new couple holding someone's baby, the new couple in each other's arms, wrapped in ski wear. The photographs worked like cue cards, she imagined, visual prompts to remind them of who they were, now, who each of them loved.

The large window in the living room exposed a street full of apartment blocks. There were few trees in the immediate vicinity and the ones that were there looked gangly and young, without majesty. There was no beauty here.

Tara stepped out of the bathroom and followed Carl throughout his circuit of the apartment, carefully watching him as he picked up the photographs. She appeared concerned, as if he might steal something from her, as if he was capable of taking the happiness out of this marriage, too.

"You're welcome to go through those boxes," Tara said, pointing to the floor.

Colleen's casserole dishes and old wedding-present crystal vases were stacked in boxes in a corner.

"Right," Colleen said, and crouched over the dishes.

◆

David watched her on her knees, sifting through his junk. "That lovely glass salad bowl was given to Tara at a shower last weekend," he said. "It's off to the Sally Ann if you can't use it."

"This is my cheese plate." Colleen held up a slab of marble.

"It's crap, Colleen."

She didn't look up. "Well, I don't know if I'd say that."

"It's crap," he said again. He enjoyed telling her this, suddenly relished her on her knees, at his feet, savored her poverty with Carl. He wanted to yell it at her, "It's crap." The whole deal's crap.

Colleen pulled a knife out of a box. She said, "I was wondering what had happened to my knives. I've been chopping with K-Tel lately."

Tara said, "Take everything."

◆

There was a capsule of Joy's mother's bath oil on the tub's edge. It was an imposition, a forced entry, but Joy wanted it. The oil as heirloom, something to soak in and return to, her mother's body. Joy took herself gently into the bath and washed off the residue from the long moving day. Everything was perfect and in its place. Nothing had broken in the move. She would be all right.

She would trace the groove her mother had made until she was comfortably settled. She would hold her breath, keep herself beneath the foamy surface. Her head would rest against the enamelled finish of the tub, legs drawn up, embryonic, until every inch of skin was safe from the cool air above.

WOMAN WITH A MAN INSIDE

Y OU DESERVE A HOME WITHOUT THE RAT," Ingrid said. "I'm going to take an apartment up the hill and give you and the girls the house."

Joy said, "He is not a rat, Mom."

Her mother said, "Do you want it or not?"

"I'll take it," Joy said.

It was the house Joy had grown up in, the street that had shaped her, for better, for worse—gangly feet bounding across sidewalk cracks, around laurel hedges, under dogwoods, into the abundant vegetable gardens, for thievery. Joy was prone to defending it, the street (but never the house itself), the way every house flaunted a fertilized green lawn, trimmed edges. Orderliness could impress her. There were times she wanted to share in it.

The first day in Ingrid's house, Joy painted a wall with four shades of green and made a blurred mural of forest trees. With a can of blue paint she mixed up a sea and surrounded the trees with it. She wanted to be loose, rough and completely unaware.

Kim and Allyson watched her with a kind of nonchalant awe. She knew they tried to have many secrets and maybe they did, though fewer than they believed.

"She's a goner without Dad." Joy heard them in their bedroom. "When's his turn?"

She wanted not to listen, but leaned toward their opened door. "Let's tell him Baskin and Robbin's. The Extravaganza." The door slammed shut. Their resistance gave Joy hope.

The girls were accustomed to long absences from their father. How different would a legal separation be? Throughout the marriage, Quaid lived in mining exploration bush camps—months at a time—and the girls were diminished to wetted mouths, living off their father's Express-posted teddy bears and postcards, waiting for his return, body and soul. When he finally did arrive home, he gave them the fullness of his bright love, his chocolate treats, his extravaganza of attention.

He and Joy made love nightly—until time came for him to return again to the rocks. His frequent absences and far-away affections had suited her. Intimacy was best had from a reliable distance. *Who honestly wants the same body around, close-up, night after night after night? The same worn terrain year after year?* He accepted this, as he accepted most things about her. She could never say he had not been supportive.

Quaid had always held fast to the hope of discovering a geologic anomaly, a mineral deposit with economic grade ore. He loved rocks, their solidity, their unending durability. Instead of monthly visits home, he used to send Joy letters filled with his plans for their future: the plot of virgin land he wanted to buy; the solar-heated geodesic dome he would one day build. He did want her feedback. Did she like the idea? Did she, too, want a geodesic dome, or virgin land? He was always using that word, given the chance. Virgin this, virgin that, virgin caesar, virgin page. It should have been no great surprise what happened.

After the separation agreement had been signed, Quaid visited daily, when not in the bush. He was a trier. When he visited the house the first time, Joy was at work in her mother's garden, planting, composting, mixing herself up with the earth in her short shorts, her legs full in the dirt.

She felt his eyes on her before he spoke. The weight of his gaze, so rare upon her skin.

Truth was, he knew his wife better by touch than by sight. She did not want to be seen close-up, particularly while making love. So, he turned off the light. He misunderstood, and she did not want to explain.

In a police line-up of masked naked women, he would be hard-pressed to identify his wife. She had accused him of this a few times. That she could even imagine such a scene—this, he said, was the real problem of their marriage.

Their former marriage. Her long thighs, the sleekness of them, the memory of them receptive and open beneath the weight of his body. She knew what he saw when he looked at her. She felt his desire, his body longing for the woman who was his wife.

He knelt beside her. "I want to make a home with you again."

"Please," she said. "Stop now." She went in the house, closed the door, the drapes. A moment passed and she peered out, watching him stand firm beside her rose bed, empty of roses. The neighbour Jack Andrews, once a friend of her father's, appeared across the street, marched down his front steps. He tipped his baseball cap at Quaid. Quaid nodded.

The two quick gestures exchanged between the men

established common ground. She understood some men. It was no problem—she had one inside her.

She'll be putty in your hands.

She knew the talk, her father and his friends.

Don't let those tight pants get to you. Wait your turn. She'll be back where she belongs in no time.

Joy closed the drape and slid down the muralled wall onto the floor, knees up and apart. She thought of them, the men, looking upon her. Everything was tight.

She concentrated on the following: roast chicken, lemon potatoes, bean salad, prep time: 30 minutes. The men vanished easily. She had a kind of control.

Quaid returned a week later to visit his daughters for an afternoon. As he left, he put his hand on Joy's shoulder. His fingers rubbed into her suncreamed skin. She kept digging. Weeds. Grass. Worms. Her hands in the dark soil with the slugs, bits of composted egg shells and carrots. A flat of Super Cascade petunias lay waiting for transplanting. She wanted to reach, no gloves, and witness her hands inside a beginning, to start from seed, to be returned, ungardened, never domesticated.

She watched his shoes walk back to his car. She listened to the car start up and rev, then unexpectedly switch off.

She was forced to look up.

Jack Andrews stood beside the driver's window, talking to Quaid. Both men looked in her direction. She was predisposed to this feeling—knowing the aim and intensity of men's eyes around her. But this *was* really happening. They *were* looking.

Quaid revved up again, jumped into gear, and was gone.

Jack Andrews strolled across the street toward her. He even moved like her father. She really had not counted on seeing him, his form, so often.

Her father and Jack had been strange bedfellows, to be sure. Joy's father was the neighbourhood's hippy artist, King of Nude Sunbathing. Andrews had a buzz-cut and bulging arm muscles. They shared, however, the same shape—short, broad torso and long striding legs.

Mr. Andrews took this occasion to lay down some rules. He made it his business to expect the street cleaning crew. He said this as he handed a notice to her, instructing the bearer to park elsewhere for the day, so that West Sixteenth Avenue could be soaped up, brand-spanking new.

"I'll be placing the notices on the windshields of all local cars. I watch over the place, the block."

"I see."

"Your father," Mr. Andrews said. "He's well, I hope."

"Yes." *Why not think of him?*

"He wrote me a postcard not long ago," Mr. Andrews said. "Could not believe it. England! Sent a computer code as his return address!"

"He doesn't like to miss out," Joy said.

Mr. Andrews and her father, once the magnates of the neighbourhood. He had been a good man, her father. Certainly he had. Together he and Andrews had arranged neighbourhood hockey games, built a communal swing on the boulevard's giant oak. Although one voted NDP and the other Social Credit, they both kept track of kids who had lost their house keys, were both aware of the comings and goings of strangers. They pruned trees and rosebushes and enjoyed the domestication of nature, even though her father maintained a defence of pesticide-free gardening.

Always, neighbours gave them the finest fruit from their gardens. Who did not love them?

In his first letter to Joy, postmarked from Bristol, her father had announced that he was newly engaged to a forward-thinking woman from home, meaning Bristol. This news Joy was expected to give her mother. A year had passed since either had seen him.

She could not speak to her mother about this passage in her father's life. Her mother was not a listener. She did not want to know.

And so it went. Her father began to surface, looming benevolently in early morning dreams. She did tell her mother this much, and her mother reminded her that dreams were scientifically irrelevant, "like the brain's way of passing gas. Only narcissists, like your father, indulge in such foolish considerations."

He appeared at Joy's bedroom door as she, a girl, prepared to undress for bed, to say that he had noticed a button missing from her blouse, and that she should leave it in the sewing bin for her mother to mend in the morning. *He was no ogre. He never laid a hand. Get real.*

Sometimes she used to avoid her father's eyes, tried not to be the object of his curiosity. Other days, she found his gaze comforting, the way he took such an interest, unlike her mother, who was always on the way out, it seemed.

At the breakfast nook, he sat across from her as she ate. Staring and smiling, just that. He told her things about herself, as if he knew her better than anyone. She was his. He made her. He fed her.

When she was fourteen she determined (by observing other girls' fathers) that her father was special, the way his eyes followed her every movement, the way he and his friends talked about… well…bodies. They were liberated! You could call it that. When she began to wear clothes in layers, they reminded her not to hide herself:

The body beautiful!

Let it all hang out, baby.

Joy, her father said, *one day you're going to have to let some young buck get a better look at you. It's nature's way.*

He said this to the nodding approval of his friends, who sat around the kitchen table drinking Inka. Against the bright window behind the men, delicate prisms hung, casting shards of bent light.

Her mother always left when the art friends arrived.

In front of mirrors, Joy began to see herself as her father saw her. It seemed necessary.

You'll feel better without a bra. Bras are out.

Women will kill for a shape like yours. You'll be an hourglass. Know what those are? 36-26-36.

Her father said, *Get your mom to measure you and we'll record your progress. Ingrid used to be one curvy lady. What a shape, man. A goddess.*

The boys are going to be lining up for you one day soon.

What if this were actually true? Or what if it turned out to be completely untrue? She did not know which was the worse future. Maybe this is the father's role, to foster her chances at successful romance. When she did wear short shorts, the artist men who were gathered there in the kitchen sang their approval, rated her progress:

Youth is wasted on the young.

Some lucky guy. There goes Eve!

It was fun, almost, standing there. And then she wanted to run like mad.

When her father couldn't tell her something about herself, he wanted her to expose a detail he may have missed. Many evenings he asked what she had eaten at each meal, and then he tallied up her day's intake: "Caraway toast and jam, a bowl of Aspen, then…let me see if I can remember. Lentil soup for lunch and Mexican cheese pie, salad and green beans for dinner. Did you have a frozen yogurt? I'll bet it was really good. What flavour?"

Joy thought he was asking her what she had eaten to see how much she was costing them in food, but it became apparent that the cost did not concern him. It was something else. He wanted to know what she was digesting, what was going on *inside her.*

Joy couldn't explain her problem to anyone; she couldn't call it anything. She mentioned her father's interest in her diet to her mother. It sounded absurd.

Her mother believed in predictability. "So he asks you what you eat? He's taking care of you as he should."

Joy gave her mother many chances to become another person. She tried to have her mother alone for discussions about the innuendos, but it seemed her father was almost always nearby, inside his wife's shadow at every chance.

He might say to Ingrid, curled on the sofa, "Yin, here's Yang."

"Oh, so there you are," her mother said, laughing, glancing quickly at Joy then back to her book. Her father read—usually an organic gardening journal—at the other end of the sofa. Under their bed were stacks of *Playboys* and the ones in which men urinated into naked women's mouths.

Joy had read them all, of course. It was effortless, really, to become a woman who takes a man inside her and leaves him there, peering out at the woman in the mirror, inhabited. It was survival.

When she asks her mother to remember her own bedroom, the state of it, her mother is a sealed vessel. Did nothing bother her? Ingrid tells her this: Her husband was not always this way. He used to wear shirts with collars, pressed slacks with cuffs. He polished his shoes. He loved to sketch and was an avid rose gardener. He ate simple British foods for dinner, drank moderately with friends at the pub, accompanied Ingrid to matinees. But he was never one to miss out. His sketching led him to art college, which further led him to the doorsteps of many young models. Nudes in particular.

She had done her best with what she had. She loved having Joy. Without Joy, Ingrid's life would have been nothing. Still, she would not tolerate ingratitude for the privileges of Joy's life. She would take no criticism. *He never laid a hand on you—that's the main thing. You learned a lot about the natural world from that man.* The rest was silence. And even if there was more, Ingrid would not hear it.

Now, morning after morning, Joy planted herself in the garden. To grow all over it, wild, weedy, herself a spray of colour and light. But she kept buying bedding plants from the super-market—the ready-made garden. This time, a flat of lobelia and mixed nikkis waited.

The neighbour Andrews approached her yet again, this time with a mower. He said, "I show good will toward everyone by mowing their lawns for free. I figure we all deserve carpet quality."

"If you'd like to cut the grass, you're welcome."

She watched Andrews regard her. *Tough Broad, you need to come down a notch.* The lines on Andrews' face spoke clearly enough.

She walked onto the carport, trying to throw him. But with each of his cool gestures, he moved further over her, on top of her shadow. He stopped at the toolshed door and pointed to the tall willow on her lawn.

"You'll excuse me," she said.

"That tree's growing wild," he said. "Needs trimming."

She imagined calling Quaid: *Get this man off my property, Mother's property.* Amicable relations, they had both agreed to it. The failure of their marriage had never been his fault, no matter how it looked. Not really. She was the one who had never been honest about her desires.

Moving toward the phone, she saw Quaid taped to the fridge in a photograph taken last summer; she regarded the glint of his scalp, the entire top of his head. Beside him, eight-year-old Kim bent in concentration over her bike, the loose chain. Kim had posted the photo the day they moved in.

You belong to our girls, that is who you are. She wants to say this to him: *It almost worked. We almost made it work. Isn't that what happened?*

She opened the fridge. The girls appeared beside her and clamoured over the stove elements.

"I miss the old mornings," Allyson said. It was the first of such comments, the impossible new beginnings.

"The way he used to make us all a glass of Indian tea," Kim continued.

"You make good tea now," Joy said.

"Yeah, but it's not home," Kim said.

"I know," Joy said. "I know this isn't your real home." She went to the closet and pulled a jacket off a hanger and onto her back, aware of her fingers, unsteady, forcing the buttons through the holes. They were crowding her in that kitchen, their expectations too loud in that kitchen.

"Mom, don't." Kimberly, the adult concern on her face.

"Just a brief foray into the light of morning."

"What?" Kimberly's pitch rising. "That doesn't help things," she said, "when you talk that way."

"Ten minutes," Joy said. "And I'll be back with a plan about the tea. Okay?"

Neither of her daughters looked at her as she went out. The door slapped against the frame. She was grateful for the way they deliberately refused to observe her.

Across the street, the evenly pleated drapes in Mr. Andrews' living room window opened and closed. Whether he was there or not was irrelevant.

I want something else. She said this to herself. She returned to the house, determined to give her girls a competent mother, someone they could depend on. They were not to worry.

"I'm back," Joy said.

"You were never here," Kimberly said. "We've agreed to forget the morning."

Allyson nodded and stared at the toaster, making faces at her reflection. There were few mirrors in the house.

Daily, Joy stood at the front window. Jack Andrews marched along the boulevard, sipping from a coffee mug.

"Mom," Allyson said. "You're acting like a statue standing there."

Possibly this was true. She had been staring at the street a lot. To endure your opponent's gaze, you take him inside your body, and observe him from the inside out. Then you know what to watch for.

He entered his neighbours' porches, or secretly penetrated their gardens with bulbs or fertilizer, and Joy stood guard, monitoring his advance.

She hid from him. She used the invisibility techniques she had developed as a teenager. At fifteen she had done her reading in a variety of hiding places—under her bed, or crouched against the side of the house where she could not be detected unless he leaned out the window. This was also a good place to overhear her father's conversations, to keep tabs on his visitors.

They talked about the women they knew, which one was the most desirable, body and soul (Mia), who opposed free love (Sandra), who had the most juice (Avril). They debated the value of strip joints. Were they disrespectful of women? They concluded that the girls were hardworking and in it for capitalist reasons. A kind of Women's Lib, they supposed. They debated the value of mushroom manure in vegetable gardens, the European sense of design as compared to the American, the legacy of Lichtenstein and Pollock in the New York art scene. Why not treat the female body as an art form, too? Why not study nude, sunbathing women? It was an act of appreciation, to enter an object by means of close scrutiny.

Now she read the morning newspaper behind the book-shelves in the living room. She wrote her covering letters for job applications while sitting on the floor, out of Jack Andrew's line of sight. As the days passed, she identified herself as paranoid, but then reasoned that she was simply cautious.

When making tea or cooking dinner, she stood against the fridge where he could not watch her and she could breathe. Her father used to instruct her mother into the kitchen, detail the ideal method for washing salmonberries, how not to knead the whole-wheat pastry. He liked pies made late at night, so that in the morning they'd be just that little bit firm. Sometimes he woke up Joy to suggest that her mother could use a bit of help in the kitchen, stuffing berries into pie shells. He stood in the doorway, sipping his warm milk, smiling only at Joy.

Something was wrong, and it had no name.

She and her mother finished the pies. The house quieted, everyone appeared to be asleep, and then she'd hear him. The dull hum of the TV in his den. His body hovering between the kitchen, the den and the bathroom, night after night.

It should have worked then, with Quaid, for he was never the same body around night after night. He could never take her fully under his scientifically trained eyes. But rather than a solution, Quaid's prolonged absences became their problem.

Why a babysitter, though? It was an embarrassing cliché

from a drugstore novel. Why right under her nose? Had he wanted her to watch? Had he wanted to be seen by her, fully, wholly, no matter what?

Joy had always treated Quaid as she had wished to be treated herself, which meant she never looked at him for very long. Particularly when he was naked. She wanted to promote a respect for privacy. The body was a private place after all.

He had found her averted eyes hurtful.

He must have set up his affair so that she would see him. She had been due home at 1:00 p.m., and he had known it. At exactly 1:00 p.m., above the dark bed sheets, Quaid's long naked ass rose like a moon, its surface slightly mottled. Up and down. He moved between the legs of an enthusiastic teenager, who yelped when she caught sight of the observer at the bedroom door.

Quaid had been seen by his wife.

She had no desire to be the observer. So she moved out.

After a month of living in her mother's house again, she received two letters from Bristol. One listed the names of her new forty-year-old stepsisters, Jude and Claire, along with the names of their children and husbands. The other letter suggested that she pack up the brood and travel to England. *I can't wait to see you again.*

That same day Quaid visited. The girls were in school. Joy decided not to mention her father's letters. Instead she talked about the neighbour.

Quaid said, "Don't go rabid on me."

"The guy is sick." She insisted. "He's always peering around."

"Sick?" Quaid said. He took a long sip from the instant coffee she had made him. "Okay, you could be right."

Don't be the teacher's pet, Q-Tip. That is what she thought. *Don't think, as you're doing right now, that siding with me about the neighbour is going to get you places.*

She opened her makeup bag and brushed mascara onto her lashes in her compact mirror. She looked herself over. *Who has the most juice?*

Quaid's eyes watered. "Jesus, I just want to make a home with you. Tell me, is that a crime?"

She said, "No, that is definitely not criminal activity."

She followed his eyes on her breasts. With each breath, she felt her breasts rise. Intake, intake. Out. Her heart pushed against the walls of her body. She saw what he saw. She felt his desire.

She felt her own desire for her own body rise within her. She led him by the hand.

Afterward, he sat naked on the bed's edge, stretching his hand toward her, expressing a rough desire for something that may never have existed between them. The weight of him had been calming to her. He was beautiful still, she could not deny it. She wanted to want him, but did not.

She felt herself flaccid, frustrated. He would not really look hard at her.

She did not know how to tell him to gaze upon her, to stand over her, unthreatening yet omnipresent, judgmental, assigned to rate her progress while she, on her knees, performed careful acts of the everyday. She did not know how to tell him to come watch her perform upon herself, to satisfy them both. He could not understand any of this, which was, of course, why she had loved him.

Her body stood lithe, waiting for something.

She said, "I'm going to take a bath."

"In private?" he said.

"Yes."

But of course she was lying. Nothing was reparable.

He took the message.

She closed the bathroom door behind her, ran the water, poured the bubbles in. She bent over the tub.

She could feel them now. Behind her, the men stood invisible, fully clothed in a line-up. She sat in the water. They did not undress. They came only to observe her technique with close scrutiny—and would not be kept waiting. She gave her fingers to herself, to no one else.

They stood over her, hard and watchful. Some muttered their approval and wanted to have a go, bringing the show to its highest point—and then to its consummate vanishing end.

III

MOTHERLAND

THE WAITING ROOMS

MICHELLE SAW HER OWN HAND WADING IN AN unflushed toilet bowl. She knew she was growing desperate. There was no logical reason for her fingers to be scaling the enamel edges of her friend's bowl. The water there was too cold to sustain life. The sperm were probably all dead.

After almost thirty seconds of fishing in the bowl, she heard the small diamond on her engagement ring clink against the vial, which was lying at the bottom near the chute. She rescued the vial, washed it with warm water and stuffed it back in her underpants. Maybe a few thousand lived, she thought. Even a hundred would do.

Driving to the Clinic at the university, she tried not to blame herself. The accident had been half Steven's fault, after all. If he hadn't thrown the vase, her stomach wouldn't have swelled from nervousness, and the accident wouldn't have happened, and all fifty million would have lived.

Fifty million, no more. His sperm count was one-quarter that of the average Canadian male. She wanted to defend him to the world, though no one had accused him of anything. *He's athletic. He's passionate and good in bed, for God's sake.*

For God's sake. Even when the words weren't spoken, she

could hear their echo, rebounding, reminding her that it might be for God's sake that she couldn't carry anything anymore. God punishes. That's what some of the old women in the congregation told her. *God punishes.*

She had excommunicated herself. No one was going to punish her for the vacuum aspirator that had tugged on her cervix in the clinic years ago. But God was not easy to forget. He'd been chained around her neck for years, hanging from a gold crucifix. They had been married for two years and had been trying for three, and in that time she had conceived and miscarried twice. She hadn't been able to hold on to anything. Zygotes could not affix themselves to her wall. She did not know who to blame. Although she was embarrassed to admit it, she had wanted to be a mother since she was eight years old.

At the clinic, in the steel-blue bathroom, she reached into her underwear and then wiped the vial with a towel. The nurse waited outside the door. Timing was critical, and passing minutes meant a great deal, especially to those in the waiting room.

The nurse, whom Michelle had never seen before, took the vial from her hand and frowned. "Where have you been keeping this?"

"Down my pants, like Dr. Klein said."

"It doesn't feel as warm as it should. Did something go wrong?"

If she were to mention the toilet, the nurse would say the procedure was a waste of time. Her decreased temperature that morning had told her she was ovulating. It was day fourteen of her menstrual cycle, and it was the only time that month she had a chance. Even if there were only a few hundred.

"No," Michelle said. "Steven did it this morning. It's fresh."

"Okay then," the nurse said, leading her into one of the insemination rooms. "I'll wash and treat the sample, and in a few minutes Dr. Klein will come in and inject..."—she looked in the file—"...Steven's sperm into you."

Michelle climbed onto the examination table and crossed her legs.

"It doesn't take long," the nurse said, handing her a beige cotton gown. "Just strip from the waist down."

"I know."

She patted Michelle on the hand. "Just relax."

"I know."

The nurse closed the door behind her, taking the vial full of Steven with her. She reappeared just as Michelle was unzipping her jeans.

"Will Steven be joining you?" she asked.

"No, not this time," Michelle said. "He's not...He can't make it."

"I'm sick of doing it with a vial," Steven had yelled earlier that morning, before he smashed a wedding present against the cupboards, before Michelle's stomach started to contract and rumble.

"It's not my fault," she had yelled back.

"Nobody said it was," Steven said.

God punishes. The congregation echoed.

"We've made love almost every night this week," she said. "It's only once a month that you've got to..."

"Masturbate!" He shoved the vial in her hand.

"Is that so bad?" she asked.

"I don't like to be forced into it."

"No one's forcing you, Steven."

"You are."

"I'll do it with you next time. I'll do it for you."

He picked pieces of the vase off the floor. "You'd better go, or you'll be late."

Her stomach clenched, bowels knotted. She stuffed the vial down her underpants and climbed in the truck to drive to the clinic. Halfway there she realised she couldn't bear the pressure in her stomach. If she didn't find a bathroom, she would never make it to the clinic clean. She stopped at a friend's, climbed through a window and ran for the toilet. Only once she'd relieved herself did she remember the vial.

Dr. Klein entered and asked Michelle to put her feet in the stirrups and to slide her bottom down to the edge of the table. From between her legs he smiled at her. He rolled a clear plastic glove over his right hand and lifted the folds of beige cloth between her legs.

"Just relax," he said, inserting his finger and probing at her cervix. "Wider, now," he told her.

She opened. The syringe filled with Steven entered her body. She closed her eyes and imagined sex with him. Normally, he would have sat beside her in that room, telling her it would be a beautiful baby. She visualized the sperm penetrating the egg. Someone told her that doing this would greatly increase her chances.

"Don't move until the nurse tells you to. You know the routine, Michelle. Twenty minutes on your back. I'm going to start you on estrogen suppositories."

"Sure," Michelle said. All this for some forty-nine million

dead sperm.

Dr. Klein patted her on the head. "Good luck," he said, shutting the door.

She heard the congregation and told them to piss off.

The following day she waited in her office. Waited for what? She was not sure. At ten o'clock the maintenance supervisor was due to arrive with his weekly report. At two minutes past ten, she waited for her boss to approach her open door, tear off the plaque which read, Michelle Carson, Hospitality Liaison, and say, You're too distracted—I'll have to fire you. At five past ten, she waited for a sign, either of conception or failure. The last thought carried her into the twelfth hour.

She walked into the staff room, hoping to chat about gardening, politics or athletes. People asked her if she and Steven were having any luck. They were waiting to hear the happy answer.

She left the staff room to the sound of broken sentences, tumbling words like tragic, difficult, waiting...forever.

She boarded the elevator, got off on the fifth floor and decided to spot check a room. In 507, she noted on her assessment pad that the fridge was stocked, the soap was fresh, the bedspread was flat with crisp edges, and the carpet didn't suggest smells of anything illegal. Under the bed was a wrapper. A rip through the gut of the horse on the cover. Extra Protection with Spermicide. It had been a long time since she had actually wanted to use one.

She was seventeen; the boy was eighteen. They had spent the afternoon exploring each other on a girlfriend's spare bed.

"I'll pull out of you before I come," he had said. "We don't need a condom."

"Okay," she had said, so agreeable.

Eight weeks later, when she repeated her doctor's words to some women in her congregation, they looked at the ground, said the choice was not hers to make. "God punishes," they warned. "God will not forget."

She was being punished now, Michelle believed. She had lost her only chance at a child.

She stuffed the wrapper in her suit pocket.

Tina, a teenaged reservations clerk, stood over her, holding a newspaper.

"Excuse me," Tina said. "I cut this out for you."

"Government Appeals to Public," Michelle read. "Foster Parents Needed Immediately. Children aged six months to sixteen years in need of temporary care."

"I thought the six months part might interest you," Tina said, twirling the heel of her shoe deep into the thick pile. "Lots of women get pregnant once they adopt. There's lots of Third World kids waiting for homes. I guess you know that. Anyway, maybe if you adopt a kid, you'll get pregnant."

"I don't think so, Tina."

"I know this is real personal stuff, but have you ever thought of getting one of those surrogate mothers?"

Quality fertile soil. Guaranteed produce. No way.

Michelle smiled her Hospitality Liaison smile. "Thank you for caring, Tina, but you'll have to excuse me. I really need the bathroom."

Every room is a waiting room when you're always waiting. Her office, the staff room, suite 507, the bedroom she shared with Steven, their kitchen, the laundry room, the study, the bathroom. Each room was a depot for her impatience. Each room was a holding tank. No matter what she was doing, one small part of her was waiting for something to happen or not to happen.

In her bathroom at home, on Day Twenty of her cycle—eight days before her period was due—she felt an ache in her lower left side. Her period had not started, but things were moving that way. In a week she would receive the monthly answer. The voices she could not talk out of her head chanted loudly. *For God's sake.*

In the kitchen, Steven dipped a strip of bread into a soft-boiled egg.

"We're both casualties of myths," she said. "Eat oysters. Have sex lying sideways. Adopt and grow fertile. Visualize the sperm. Do it in the bathtub. Don't drink coffee. Caffeine decreases fertility. Gain weight. You need fat cells to conceive."

"Don't cry, Michelle."

"It's coming. I can feel it."

"Next month. Next month."

"Never," she said.

Michelle sat on the hardwood floor and took the Yellow Pages between her legs. Steven crouched beside her and said, "Let me do it." His fingers scanned the physicians' pages. They looked for a name they didn't recognize. Doctors who knew Michelle hesitated to give her a Blood Pregnancy Test. But a blood test is the only kind to have, Michelle thinks. Forty-eight hours after conception it knows. Urine isn't as smart.

"Just wait a little longer," the familiar doctors said to

Michelle. "It's an expensive test to keep running. What's a few more days?"

Forty-eight hours, Steven said.

He dialed Dr. Singh and asked for an appointment. The doctor obliged Michelle, wrote out a blood test requisition while mentioning the rising cost of health care in this province. In the lab she watched the needle fill, withdrawing her purple blood, withdrawing the waiting. Tomorrow, she would be freed from it. She sighed and offered the lab technician some gum.

The next morning she knelt on the floor beside the phone, sipping hot milk. Steven stood against the stove when the phone began to ring. He did not move.

She did not rush to answer it. She did not rush to know.

PHILIPA OF HARARE

T HE NAME WAS TO BE HER PASSPORT TO FORTUNE. In the hospital nursery the plan had been this: a member of the Royal Family—male, single, and born before 1961—would think fondly and instantly of his father Prince Philip the moment his ears were graced with the sweet sound of "Philipa," a ravishing but obedient commoner from the colonies.

Here lay the rest of Maureen's job—to raise her daughter obedient, to foster a passionate countenance in the girl (Royals like a bit of spunk in their women, she had read), and finally to orchestrate the unlikely meeting between a prince and the wee babe nestled in bright pink blankies, bassinet number seven, Lucky Seven, on the third floor maternity wing, St. Paul's Hospital.

The meeting *seemed* impossible from her current stand-point beside the nursery window in St. Paul's, she knew. But strange happenings were daily occurrences as far as she could see. Open any newspaper, she would say. Listen to my life. Or head down to the docks and chat up the fishermen. They'll all tell you about miracles on the sea. She had done this a few times herself, gone down to the docks and even experienced one—a miracle, that is. She and Bill Dunlevy, a hired hand on a large

115

troller, the first time they made love, a miracle occurred.

Why should her plans for their baby not be subject to the world of daily miracles? Although it was not obvious that Philipa would be a beauty, there was no cause for concern. Maureen knew how to make do with what God had given. Maureen would teach her daughter how to apply makeup to enhance the cheekbone, how to lighten her eye lids (Philipa's lids did seem to droop), how to shape and colour the mouth into an unforgettable, pink O.

That's what got Bill Dunlevy in the end. He even said so. "That mouth of yours, girl, I dream about it every night. I kid you not. Your lips are perfection in heaven itself." He spoke like a prince, that's what got Maureen in the end. She even said so.

They had bedded down in Mrs. Renke's Rooms To Let, where Maureen had rented the finest flat in the house. From her tall window she took in Burrard Inlet, the industrious harbour and its grey-green water, Grouse Mountain and the Lions. Bill expressed his appreciation. His lovemaking was true to his words; he was a prince to the end.

When Maureen announced the miracle that was to occur nine months later, Bill ran. He quit the docks and disappeared from her life. Her womb grew hot and bigger by the month. She cried daily. She wept brushing her hair and teeth. She wept as she squeezed her growing body into the girdles and pinching skirts she had always worn to work. She could not write to her mother in England for help with money. Her mother already had two other daughters to raise on air as it was.

Maureen's job had been as a cashier in the Notions section of Woolworths. It paid the rent, bus fare, groceries and provided pin money. Woolworths was not a company that would permit an employee to be visibly pregnant. The Five-and-Dime could not afford to lose respectability.

Her alternate job was with White Dove Laundries. She was hired as a shirt-presser. The day she started work, two washer-women quit. She found herself working the machines, watching her beautiful gloved hands and arms deep in boiling water, lye, bleach. Something had to change or she herself was going to rip that child right out of her belly.

Maureen was on her lunch break, behind the laundry, eating her second chicken salad sandwich, drinking her second glass of milk, in between her second and third pieces of apple strudel—(her enormous body demanded more and more food, the body had even begun to eat at her)—when an apparition of Bill Dunlevy appeared, lumbering up the alley toward her. The lye had created a problem with her vision. But he, the real person, arrived with his whole body, knelt in front of her, his hand outstretched with a small green velvet box. Inside: a gold band, and on top of the band a diamond of a quarter carat. A real diamond, not the chips like most of the Woolworths girls had on their rings, but a real chunk of the rock.

The second miracle of her life: Bill came back. That she brought herself to marry and almost forgive him, the third miracle. She took the opportunity of her unexpected marriage to write her mother and invite her to visit. Mr. William Dunlevy would gladly afford his mother-in-law an airline ticket to Vancouver. She announced her marriage by signing the letter from Mrs. William Dunlevy. It was a good name. Her mother would be able to brag now about the daughter who had been sent off to Canada.

Maureen had plans to brag about her own daughter. The day after Philipa turned two years old, Maureen started taking her measurements. The calculation was this: at exactly the age of two, multiply the child's height by two and there you'll have her anticipated height at twenty-two. Maureen herself, at five foot six inches, was too tall for many men. So she was relieved to discover that Philipa would be five feet two inches at best. Her demure height would serve her well, no doubt. It would make her future husband, even if he should not be a Royal exactly, feel especially male, guaranteed pretty well of having an eight inch rise on his wife.

Philipa would have to learn to manage herself in the world of men. And ours is a world of men, make no mistake, Maureen would tell her toddling daughter. Maureen's own father had been a real man and taught Maureen the ways of men, what a man liked to come home to, how to keep him from wanting a mistress, how to break a man's arm if he is getting too fresh. Philipa however had only Bill Dunlevy with his good heart and good intentions. Bill was a bit of, how could she say, in a man's terms, a candy ass. He never gave Philipa a wallop, didn't believe in it. Not for girls.

"Well, la-de-da," she said to him. "You don't have to live with it, our girl's screaming, and gandying about, her tantrums in the SuperValu, the trinkets and such she tries to put down the toilet. Even your fine engagement band, Mr. Dunlevy!"

"She's just a baby—a female baby at that," he said. And then off Bill Dunlevy went, to the sea, for weeks on end, back for a few days, to be loved and to eat a few helpings of Shepherd's Pie, enjoy a wrestle with little Philipa, read her the odd storybook throughout the day and then, gone. He did pay the bills at least, that much she could say for him. And there were no black eyes on the female sex in the Dunlevy house.

She could only hope that the princes Andrew, Edward and Charles received similar care from their father, Prince Philip. One hoped that in a private moment among the Royals, possibly after the royal nanny had given the boys their baths, Philip (at ease, a long day of princely duties behind him) encouraged his boys to run into his arms, swept them onto his great lap and read them... well, a noble children's book. It was critical to Philipa's chances that the young princes thought positively of the name Philip. Pray the man never beat the boys, or else Philipa's name, rather than a blessing, would act as a curse, dashing any hope of her getting inside.

Hours before delivering her second child Maureen resolved not to gamble so much on the name this time, particularly if the baby was a girl. And it was.

This time she turned to the Tudors of England for guidance. Queen Mary was regarded by the history books as a most dutiful daughter, dutiful to her mother. Certainly Maureen would need a daughter like this, especially if Philipa was to be out in the world developing her passionate countenance. Mary Dunlevy might consider a career as a licensed practical nurse, help her aged mother up the stairs as well as managing the small but comfortable house Philipa hopefully would provide for them all. Bill Dunlevy accepted his wife's recommendation for the name of their second born. Our Blessed Virgin Mary, sure, why not?

Later that year, she gave birth to a third daughter, Jane (named in consideration of Jane Seymour, the one wife to give

Henry the Eighth a son). Maureen concluded that hooking up with a Royal was no longer of primary importance. She saw her plan for Philipa as ridiculous now and completely unlikely. There was such a thing as luck after all. Luck was something she could not control, and the Dunlevy house was not blessed with exceptional good fortune. She wrote to her mother and broke the news about the third granddaughter. *I guess my life is something like yours, Mother. I too have only daughters.*

Her mother wrote back, a rare occasion.

Mo, You're doing better than you would have here. No one I know has a clothes dryer or a twenty-six inch TV. Don't kid yourself. Moving to Canada was a good thing. I wish I didn't get sea sick. I wish I didn't have a fear of flying. There's none of those supermarkets you wrote about here. Every day, I still have to go to the butcher then to the greengrocer. Tiring. Canada sounds lovely. The girls are darlings. The snaps are lovely. Keep them coming. Phillipa looks a solid lass. I was too hard on you when you were a girl, sending you off to one of the colonies. It was only a cheap angora sweater that you nipped from Mr. Hughes' Woolens Shop. Who knows? Maybe the old sod deserved it. Forgive me. Love, Mom.

Who the hell was she trying to kid? For one, she couldn't even bother to spell Philipa's name properly. What was this compulsion to add an extra L? Two, calling Philipa solid was a snipe if Maureen ever heard one. Might as well have called her a horse.

Bill Dunlevy, for initially shirking his paternal responsibilities, leaving nineteen-year-old Maureen to go it alone and work while pregnant, in a laundry, was being cursed with daughters. A fourth child would only bring another girl into the family, Maureen knew. The extraordinary events in the Dunlevy house were now termed phenomena. There were no more miracles. There would be no male heir. Still, there was no reason not to prepare Philipa for some kind of greatness. Any millionaire would do now. Prince or no prince.

At Philipa's seventh birthday party, however, Maureen noted, in a brief moment between feeding baby Jane in the high chair and chasing after Mary, making sure she didn't take another tumble down the concrete stairs (Bill never got around to carpeting them), and handing out hot dogs to the grade two girls, that Philipa was not a beauty. The phenomenon of Philipa's plainness. This was confirmed as Maureen compared Philipa to each of the other girls around the decorated table, the other little princesses in their yellow hair-bows.

Maureen decided she was going to step in. The following week she told Bill. Enough reading together on the sofa—what exactly was that going to prepare her for, except more reading? Philipa needed to be prepared, now, by a woman in a man's world.

Bill told her to go easy on the girl.

Maureen and Philipa took the bus to Simpson's Modelling Agency. Yes, they could work on her slouch and her walk. The makeup classes didn't start until a girl turned twelve, but that was no reason not to learn now how to walk, how to stand, and how to sit. These were not natural skills as most people believed. There was a way to sit and a way not to sit. The agency assured Mrs. Dunlevy: seven-year-old Philipa was in the right hands. They would even keep a portfolio on hand for clients needing child models.

Hundreds of dollars were invested in poise and grooming

classes by the Dunlevys at the Simpson's Agency. Eventually Philipa was called to be one of twenty boys and girls riding a carousel in an advertisement for the Pacific National Exhibition. The ad, which was plastered on many city buses, showed the smiling faces of seven children and the left hand and leg of Philipa Dunlevy. Her face was behind her horse. Mrs. Dunlevy, defeated, withdrew her daughter from the agency.

Some years passed. Seven years, in fact. Maureen did not have the time or inclination to forward Philipa's modelling career. Ten-year-old Mary was a difficult child and took up all of Maureen's energy. Bill was home now two nights a week and one of those was often spent making love to his wife. Maureen still enjoyed his fine body, and he seemed to enjoy hers. As it happened sex was the highlight of her week. He was still her prince, and this was some kind of phenomenon. She did not know what she had done to deserve him really.

When all the girls were at school, Maureen brought in sewing work—hems, sleeve lengthenings, button holes and the like. The one aspect of her work she did not like was that anyone could drop by at any time. She was not always ready. She tried to keep a tube of lipstick by the door at all times, but on occasion Mary nipped it and Maureen was forced to find a way to make her lips into what they should be all the time, the unforgettable pink O. She had been known to use Pink Coral nail polish in a pinch. Quick as she could, she'd paint it on her lips, straighten her dress and answer the door. This was to instill confidence in her customers, not have them wondering whether this rag-tag woman would be able to sew an even hem.

For the non-whites she did extra and never charged for it. For the young black men in particular, not that there were many who came to her for mending, she took care of everything. If she saw a hole in a jacket or sweater on their backs, she'd say, 'it won't take a minute, sit down and have a cup. I'll patch it.' She assumed most of the blacks were foreigners and poor. Helping them in her own small way was a respectable route to heaven. She had been thinking of heaven a great deal lately, thinking of a good long rest. She wanted to make sure there would be one at the end of all this.

If a black man happened to be in the house when Philipa came home from school, Maureen shooed her into the bedroom. "Don't want him getting all excited at the sight of you," she whispered.

"Why not?" asked Philipa.

"It's a cruel thing to tease a man."

"What?" Philipa was incredulous.

"Don't be disobeying me. I haven't been feeling well for weeks now."

After the customer left, satisfied (but always suspicious it seemed), Mrs. Dunlevy talked to Philipa about men, household chores, and the value of education—of which there was little. The main thing was to take care of herself financially, which meant finding a good man. Maybe she too should think about going down to the docks when she got a bit older. Maybe she, too, would get lucky.

That afternoon Mrs. Dunlevy's depression deepened as news arrived from the doctor's office that she was pregnant for the fourth time, at the age of thirty-four, and too far along to do anything about it.

John Michael Dunlevy was born two weeks early at the

Grace Hospital. Maureen went into a paralysis of ecstacy. She stood over his bassinet for hours, simply staring at his perfection. She could hardly believe the curse had been lifted. She did not know what she and Bill had done to deserve the change in their luck. She sent a telegram to her mother: Mum. Stop. A boy. Stop. Luv Mo. Telegrams, were they not the chosen mode of communication among the wealthy? Her mother would undoubtedly be impressed. Why she could take it around the neighbourhood even.

The newspapers had begun to report that bottle feeding was inferior to breast. While her girls were babies the doctors had said the opposite. So she nursed him. He kept her with him day and night. They were a right pair, mother and son. They were complete.

Once the clarity surrounding John's infancy lifted, Maureen turned her attention to the implications of the birth. Miracles were back in. They were coming her way again. She had read last week in *The Courier* that Prince Philip, Queen Elizabeth and their son Andrew would be at a parade next Saturday. God was looking kindly upon the Dunlevys now. Couldn't hurt, really, to give it a try.

◆

Phil Dunlevy took the rollers out of her hair too early. The brown strands clumped together and drooped heavily. *This is fucking ridiculous*, she mouthed into the mirror as her mother went into the bathroom to find the curling iron.

Phil took a drag from her cigarette and examined herself, edged closer to the mirror and drew the baby-blue eye shadow crayon across her lids. *Okay, I look good.*

Her mother returned with the crimson-coloured, floor-length satin dress that Phil had worn as a bridesmaid at her cousin's wedding.

"You're joking," Phil said.

"Do I look like I'm joking?" her mother said.

"I'm not doing it. You're going too far."

Her mother said, "You're still a child. You're only fourteen." She unzipped the dress and slipped it over Philipa's head. "I let you get away with too much."

It was a wet spring morning in a privileged neighbourhood on the west side of Vancouver. The main street, naturally, had been closed. Phil stood at the front, right at the curb. Her crimson taffeta shoes were soaked with the wet cherry blossoms that had been rained off the boulevard trees earlier that morning. The street was covered rather perfectly with pink blossoms, as if God himself had decorated the street for the Royal Family. Phil knew that's how her mother would have seen the day. Her mother's eyes were unfortunately set directly behind her own eyes, inside her own head.

It did not take long for the Royal motorcade to approach. She did as her mother had advised. She stood right on the curb—to give her a bit of height—held her head high and looked directly at the Prince named Andrew, who was her age. She had been instructed to smile. She smiled. She had been told to speak loudly and clearly, *My name is Philipa*, but only if he noticed, only if their eyes caught. The prince named Andrew did look at her. He held his gaze right on her. She could hardly believe it. He smiled. My god, she thought, a prince is smiling at me. Me, Philipa Dunlevy.

He looked her over.

She whispered, "My name is Philipa."

The motorcade drove on, past the major intersection, then turned right. The prince did not turn around.

She looked down, examined the crimson dress that covered her body. She was ready to kill her mother.

Across the street, Gold's Fabrics drew her attention. Phil asked a sales clerk if she could borrow a pair of scissors. She cut the dress from a maxi into a midi, sheared off the cap sleeves, and lit her last cigarette. She threw her empty Du-Maurier package into a waste basket.

On the street most of the crowd had fallen away, single file, window shopping, or waiting for the bus. No great shakes. Really, nothing had happened, except a blonde boy, wearing a string of puka shells around his neck, was approaching her now.

"Philipa?" he said.

"Yeah?"

"Philipa, that's a cool name."

"What?" She felt her underarms spring.

"Whatever you're doing with that gown of yours, hacking it up. I can dig it."

"You can?" He was grade eleven or grade twelve, she wasn't sure. "How do you know my name? You go to Kits?"

"I got a car. I can give you a ride."

"No, thanks." *But you're pretty damned cute.*

"I heard you say your name at the parade." Then he whispered, "My name is Philipa."

Shit, she thought.

"I got some grass. What do you say?"

When she arrived home, she was still high. Her father had

little John out in the back alley, learning how to hit a puck. Her mother was nowhere obvious. She snuck in the front door, bagged the destroyed dress, slipped into her Seafarers and a peasant blouse. She brushed her hair and reapplied her makeup. This sexy look would earn her few hassles from her mother. *Don't sell yourself short.* By this her mother meant don't sleep with someone who isn't going to get you anywhere. *Shoot for the top. Don't bother with the gutter. Put out for the right man and riches will come.*

Jane stood at Phil's bedroom doorway and said, "I'm going to tell Mom." She pointed to the bag that held the former dress.

Phil said, "You do and I'll tell your friends about the time you peed your pants in the elevator at Eaton's." This kind of threat was enough to terrify Jane into silence. Mary, however, was another matter. She had to steer clear of Mary.

Jane, in an uncharacteristic moment, ran at her. "I never wanted to be like you... or Mom. I hate you."

"What do you mean, like me or Mom? We're totally different."

"You both gob on makeup and wear stick-up bras."

"Push-up bras, push-ups," Phil said. "At least get your insults right. Jesus F-ing Christ, someone around here should get things right."

Her mother arrived home later that day with Mary. She shoved Mary through the front door and said, "Your room." Mary's hands were tied behind her back.

Mary said, "So, are you moving to England?" Then she collapsed laughing.

Phil thought about kicking her in the head.

"A store detective called me an hour after you left," her mother said. "He caught Mary at The Bay, pinching a bloody Mood Ring of all things." Mary was guided into her bedroom. "Stay," her mother said. And then turning away from Mary's door, "Well?"

"He didn't look at me," Phil said.

"Not once?"

"No."

"I hope you smiled." Her mother poured two shots of scotch. "You know why I chose your name."

"You think I don't know?"

"I guess it's a done thing then."

"I met a boy," Phil said, trying to ease her mother's heart for a day. "His parents are rich."

Puka Man, or Richard as she called him to his face, had driven her from the parade to his house in Shaughnessy, the tightest neighbourhood in Vancouver. A real broomstick-up-your-butt neighbourhood and loaded. He said his parents were out all day. He said he could do whatever he wanted at home.

His home was some kind of African art gallery. In every room there were images of Africa: antelope horns above the sofa, the skin of a leopard on the hallway wall, metal plates with drawings of tall skinny men chasing animals lined up on a dark cabinet.

She and Richard sat on a hand-woven rug, smoked two joints and looked through his family photo albums. Stacks of albums full of safaris, men and women in khaki shorts, black children smiling in dugouts, white women in sturdy walking sandals with knapsacks on their backs. Red soil, giraffes, elephants, lions. Phil saw herself suddenly in an episode of *Born Free*. She saw Richard beside her, he too in khaki shorts, mending the leg of a lame lion.

They smoked more grass and drank rum and cokes. She saw them on a safari, a zebra crossing in front of their jeep. A lioness and her cubs. Moving deeper and deeper into the worlds of the photo albums, Phil saw magic.

There were no Captain Crunch cereal crumbs in the albums or milk stains on the table, no Ban Roll-on (presumably no one cared about such superficiality), no scotch decanters (who'd need it in a place like that?), no bags of makeup or crimson dresses. There were herds of animals. There was Africa.

Richard put his hand on her breast and said, "You want to see my room?"

They went at it like animals. She thought this would appeal to him, considering the kind of places he was used to. But he seemed more interested in watching her undress, that's when he seemed most turned on. She did the breathing thing at the right time, she knew how to fake it, that was for sure.

Peek-a-Puka, Peek-a-Boo, or just plain Peeper. All were variations on Richard. He was into catching Phil sitting on the toilet, washing herself in the shower, bending over naked, putting on her socks. He liked to watch. Other than that, he was okay. She hung onto him. Her mother approved. He was a good catch, and Phil had to agree. Maybe he'd take her to Africa one day.

However, soon enough, Christmas morning arrived. Phil's

little brother John sat on his mother's lap. Not so little any more, he had just turned three. John carefully ripped the paper off his gift from Richard.

Her father said, "Give it a good rip, John."

John continued plodding, then held up a plastic rifle.

Her mother said, "Good God."

Her father said, "There's nothing wrong with guns."

Her mother, demure, playing the role of a Christmas-movie- mom, turned to Philipa and said, "Father thinks I'm too soft."

Phil said, "What?" She knew how not to laugh at the wrong time.

Jane and Mary broke into their gifts politely. They smiled and said thank you to each other.

Phil could barely stand it. The fruitcake. The International Coffee Swiss Mocha instant they were expected to drink, the walnuts they were expected to crack. It was always the fakest morning of the year.

"Very respectable occupations are to be had with guns, my love. Let's go, John. Hunt a few squirrels."

John threw down the gun and moved on to his next gift.

Jane said, "I'll bet if John were a little girl Richard would have given him a doll."

"And if I were a monkey," her mother said, "he'd have given me a banana, now what's wrong with that?"

"Easy now mother," father said. "That's a nine-year-old lass you're talking to."

Her mother said, "Philipa, you must be dying to know the contents of the little green box. When your father gave me a little green box..."

Phil opened it under her mother's full gaze. Edibaubles. This was the brand name of the baked plasticine jewelry that had recently come into vogue. Phil put a broccoli broach and apple-core earrings on the coffee table.

Her mother said, "Dump the cheap bastard." She looked closely at the Edibaubles. "A blonde rinse wouldn't hurt you in the search for the right fellow."

Her father said, "Lay off the girl."

Sometimes she couldn't breathe after her mother spoke about her future. Richard was never going to take her to Africa. And peroxide, no way. Peroxide was not in her future.

Her father said, "John, you're a big lad now. Don't need to be sitting on mommy's lap all day. Let's get away from all this girl-talk."

Her mother said, "Lay off the boy."

"He's my son."

She said, "He's my son."

How did we get here again? Phil wondered. *The boy, the boy, the boy. I am the one. It's me who's hurting. Do not cry. Do not cry.* Her eyes were welling all right, but she was getting good at holding herself in. It was working.

John said, "Philipa, Philly...you be the bear and I be the hunter."

Phil said, "Okay." She lay on the carpet and invited her brother to shoot her.

Stewardessing was her only way to Africa now. She would have to make certain to graduate from high school since stewardessing required it. She had read all about the job in the Careers–Female binder at school.

John said, "I gotta skin you now, Phil. Turn over." But he turned his gun on the fireplace.

Anyway, she told herself, maybe it's best this way. The creep wanted to watch me do it with myself. How much longer could I have put him off? If I had done it *for* him, well, then he would have known I'd faked it *with* him, every time.

Days later her mother said, "You can lie about these things on forms," when Phil mentioned her future career aspiration. "Graduation, smaduation, no one checks these things if they like you. Important thing is to impress the person interviewing you for the job. That'll get you a whole lot further than some B in Science. "

Her mother could be right. Phil really didn't know. She found a compromise in Frost 'N Tip. It was not a full peroxide job. Just a kind of brush that put streaks of blonde in her hair. Her mother seemed satisfied.

To satisfy herself, Phil kept Biology 11 notes under her bed and read them at night. She wanted to graduate. She wanted to get to Africa.

Years passed. She forgot about Africa and she could not orgasm. She slept with at least fifty men, most of whom had been her immediate supervisors or were company presidents. Still, she faked well. She left school two courses short of graduation. Her mother had been right. It didn't make any difference at the time. The day she left school she was hired by a millionaire as his personal real estate assistant and later, his mistress.

She had affairs with two other men in the office as well. She made good money, drove around in her boss's Mercedes, went to parties in black velvet dresses. She was doing all right. Sometimes she had four or five old buzzards on the go. Her mother was proud, but suggested the time was approaching for a ring. Phil would be twenty-five soon.

Her mother said, "I look forward to the day that one of you kids show me I raised you right. Even Jane, the brain, going off to university—now there's something to brag about. But what does she decide to study? Post-colonial literature? More books!"

"Oh, Mom," Phil said. "Don't talk that way." It gave her satisfaction to be kind to the old woman, and to condescend.

"None of you girls really loved your mother," her mother continued.

"Cigarette?" Phil opened her gold-plated case and offered it to her mother.

"Did Jim Creighton buy you that?"

"Uh-huh."

"Least he could do, considering what he's getting for free."

Phil said, "Shut up or I'm leaving."

"Oh, all right." She took a cigarette from Phil's case. "I miss holding Johnny. I miss watching him play Hot Rods and GI Joe down at the park. The smell of his hair after a day of playing. Now he's at some kind of boy's camp, being trained to be a boy, I guess."

"Too bad he didn't want to go," Phil said. "He even phoned me about it."

Her mother took a deep drag off her cigarette.

"Why do you two get on so well? He's always liked you."

"We're two wild animals, that's why." Phil did not know what she meant, only that it was true. "We love to, well, roar together. We're safari partners. I play his games."

"Uh-huh. Well, tell me, what kind of normal boy wouldn't want to go to camp with his da? All the more reason to send him. I just want him to be normal."

Men, boys, men, boys. Her mother, that's all she ever talked about. No surprises there.

Phil was not surprised by men either. Slow hand down her thigh, move to the crotch, a nibble on her neck, tongue inside her mouth, sometimes in other places, still none of them could surprise her into an orgasm. She had some pieces of jewelry. She didn't have a car, or her own apartment. Millionaires, some of them, and none provided her with more than free coke and the odd chip of diamond hanging on a chain.

One day Jim Creighton, her current boss, suggested she invest a few grand in a certain penny stock on the Vancouver Stock Exchange. Later that evening, she saw the film *Out of Africa*.

It was a sign, that the investment and the movie came to her on the same day.

The following morning she bought and read a book for the first time since grade 12. She discussed the film with a clerk at Coles who told her to read South African writers if she wanted to understand anything relevant about South Africa.

"No, wait," the clerk said, "wrong country. *Out of Africa* takes place near Nairobi, a city in Kenya."

"Doesn't matter," Phil said. She had gotten facts muddled before and came through all right. "I've got to start some-where."

After finishing a book on South Africa she tried to find a Canadian chapter of the African National Congress. She phoned Jane now living in Toronto. She said, "I want to get away like you did, but I'm going to go farther."

Jane said, "That's good, you've got further to go."

Phil begged for a crash course in world politics.

Jane recommended Zimbabwe writer Dambudzo Marechera first. Jane talked for an hour about freeing people from the tyranny of dominant powers, being free from internalized racism, from internalized self-deprecation. She had many things to say, but Phil could only listen for so long without confusing the whole business.

She thought briefly about becoming a spy for the ANC. She may not read so well, but she could take action. She could spy. She could risk her life. It had to be total if she was going to get out.

She listened closely to press reports of life in Zimbabwe and South Africa. When her penny stock paid off five hundred percent she told Jim Creighton what she had to do.

"I'm going to become a missionary."

"Finally," he said. "You see things my way."

"Not in bed," she said, removing his hand from her body as if he were a leper. "A real missionary. I'm going celibate."

Over the following weeks she told each and every one of the old goats about her plan. She imagined the goats at her feet, kissing her as if she were a saint. St. Philipa, was it possible? There was a movie she saw once about johns worshipping a former prostitute, who became some kind of nun.

The goats mocked her. A month later they were curious. A month after that they stopped groping her in elevators. She was a woman of mystery now. She would be loved only for her mind and heart.

None of the established organizations of mercy and good-will could use her. Peace Corps, well, she had to be American. All the dumpy Canadian equivalents required applicants to possess a university degree or experience that would be of benefit to peoples in developing nations. She could not even sew, build houses, or grow food. She could type, that was about it, really. She fantasized about attending university and becoming a professor of something useful. She began to wonder how much she had missed out on and why she had stopped reading. Where was her father? Why hadn't he insisted that she finish school? Why was Jane the one to survive the Dunlevy household? There were questions.

John and her father were roughing it at a pre-Christmas Outward Bound wilderness camp. He wouldn't have said much about her emigration anyway. He had finished with his fatherly duties regarding his first-born. Your mind's your own, he had said when she turned twenty-one. Call me Bill.

John, however, might be devastated. Youngest and oldest, they were equally passionate about the necessity for the other to exist. It was John and Phil who ruled the day, who carried the weight of their parents' hopes. They knew how to run with it.

At Christmas, Phil gathered Mary and Jane (visiting from Calgary and Toronto respectively) with their mother in the kitchen and told them about the one-way airline ticket. If she told them all at once, they could argue with each other about her plans.

Upon hearing news of the flight to Harare, her mother said, "Why not send money to World Vision and leave it at that?" She was aiming to be cool, but she was shaking.

Mary said, "You're going to leave Mom?"

Jane said, "Why would you want to situate yourself in a culture where you'll be part of the dominant minority? After everything we've discussed. It's a bit of an ego thing, isn't it, Phil?"

Phil said, "I have to go."

Her mother said, "I never understand a word any of you say anymore. Dominant minority. At least when I made off for the colonies, I went to better my lot. Salisbury, Rhodesia, that's where you're going. The standard of living is worse there, you know. You're going backwards. And you'll never blend in among the blacks."

Jane said, "Blending isn't her goal, Mother."

Phil, chaste now and a practitioner of meditation, had thoughts of killing her mother when she spoke about Phil's future. It was getting late. She really had to get on that plane.

She slept in good hotels. She went on safaris. She was the white woman in sturdy walking sandals. She saw the black children in dugouts. She wished they were her own. She was Isak Dinesen. She took up writing short stories, but did not care to finish them. She was out, out, out. Her mother was far behind. The old goats with their scaly hands were a thing of the past. She was free. Born free.

Then a letter from her mother arrived:

Dear Philipa: I remember looking into Johnny's crib, loving him so, afraid I would ruin him, and now if you only knew about the phenomenon of John's evil. He comes home from those damned nature camps and I want to give him a big hug. I can see he wants this too. That is until the last trip. Seems with you gone, he's blaming me, or he's very mad at me. Says I'm as warm as cold fish. How did my boy go bad? If you only knew the things he's up to now. Seen any wild tigers? How fascinating your life must be. Remember to stay with your own kind. The animals do, don't they? Luv, Mum.

She went to the white hotels, drank white cocktails, sat writing notes under the oranging sun in her white notebook. She talked only with white people, it seemed, and there were so few. Occasionally she spoke with blacks, but none were tourists. She only met bartenders, waiters, porters. She didn't know what to do. She did not want to be alone with all the Brits and Yanks crawling in this place. She was getting lonely. She went to the bathroom and painted her lips into an unforgettable pink O. Her luck had to turn.

He introduced himself as a school teacher from the local elementary, just blocks from the hotel. Yes, she had passed it many times. She loved to watch the children. She didn't know why really, only that she had started to want some of her own. She would not learn anything sitting in the white hotel, he told her, nothing that was worth knowing.

His father had been white, Douglas de Villiers. His mother was black and her name was Mercy. He gave his parents' names before he said his own, which was Charles. The de Villiers family, Charles continued, kidnapped his father back to South Africa when news arrived of the woman he had impregnated. He told her all this before she had finished her first cocktail. "My friend makes you a good drink?"

She could only nod. She didn't want to speak. Her mouth remained on the rim of the glass.

"The family at least sent Mother money to have me well-educated," he said to Philipa. "They did not completely abandon us."

He told her of the colonial history of the hotel she was staying at. He said things she did not understand.

He was fascinating. She thought about it, all right. She could see him in the other half of her bed.

They left the hotel after he gave the bartender a long embrace. "That man, he led me to you."

"What?" Phil said.

"I told him of this tourist woman, with very pink lipstick. He knew who I meant. I saw you looking through the fence at the school. I have been waiting for you."

All my life, Phil thought. Why not say, All of my life. And really top things off. Instead she said, "Same here."

He said, "Do not lie to me."

She said, "I have known you for exactly one hour."

He said, "I want to know you forever."

She almost told him to cut the shit. Instead she said, "Where are we going?"

"That is a profound question. It is a good question. Let me show you my city." And he did. They visited all the sights she had heard about and more that she hadn't. In the National Gallery he sounded like one of the books she had read back in Canada. "And the problematic part," he said, referring to a display of artifacts, "is that this exhibit was mounted by my people."

Here goes, she thought. God, let me say the right thing. "You want your people to be free from internalized racism?" Phil said.

"Yes," Charles said. "Precisely."

He stopped her in front of a display of dark masks. He held her shoulders and looked all over her face. "Some people, Phil, would say I'm interested in you because I want to repeat my parents' experience."

She got a good opportunity to look through him. She said, "People could say the same about me. You know, the colony thing."

"Is it true?" he asked.

"I don't know," she said. "Is it true for you?"

"I don't know."

The way he doubted himself—well, it was a total turn-on.

He, like all the other men she had slept with, could not surprise her into an orgasm. But he was intent on hopeful. He worshipped her naked with the lights on. He was not repelled by her open legs. He did not want the curtains drawn in her colonial hotel. Her only worry was that he might one day discover what a pack of idiots her family was, with the exception of Jane. If he ever met Jane, a different problem might arise. He might prefer her mind.

Phil's womb grew hot and bigger by the month. She did not cry. Charles did not run and she did not have to write to her mother for help.

Christmas morning came to her under an acacia tree. She and Charles did not drink International Coffees Swiss Mocha. They did not exchange presents. Instead they got married.

She sent a telegram home. She signed it from Ms. Dunlevy because Charles believed she should keep her own name.

Names were important to him. He was concerned about the name their child should take. She drifted off during such talks.

The first letter of congratulations came from the Vancouver

Juvenile Correctional Institute.

Dear Phil: Mom mentioned your wedding. Good timing. Took her mind off me for a while. They're calling it assault with a deadly weapon. What can I say? Shrinks say Dad is a dominant bastard and Mom abandoned me. Fuck 'em, I say. But I'm going to visit you when I rob a bank (a joke, Mr. Prison Guard). Love John.

The second letter.

Dear Phil: Congratulations from Mary, Mother and Bill, and of course I wish you well. Although the institution of marriage is historically difficult to swallow, I hope you find happiness within its confines. Maybe you and Charles will visit. Mother asked me to write. She's got the flu. She's handling it all quite well. Unfortunately you must know what I mean. I'm sure she'll come to embrace Charles in time. The irony of his first name has not been lost on her. Love, Jane.

The arrival of the second letter set off the first contractions, which were spaced carelessly throughout the hours of the day. Regularity set in that night. Charles drove her to the hospital at eight minutes apart.

The midwife told her to find an image to focus on when the pain surged.

Phil found the image somewhere deep in herself; through the nausea and this pain to die from, there it was: the bleeding sun and a lioness lounging with her cubs. *Born Free.*

The doctor said, "Find a chant to help you concentrate."

It was there. *Born Free. Born Free. Born Free.*

The doctor guided a head out between her legs.

Was there any such place on earth as *Born Free?*

The midwife washed the blood and cream off his new body and lay the perfection on her stomach. Charles's arms moved around her shoulders, already taking the boy in. She held the unnamed boy closely, closely but not tight.

YOU ARE MINE

SHE HAD NAMED HIM AFTER THE SUN. He would bring light to her when she was alone in the night. He would be her sun ray; her son, Ray. She would give to him her love of trees, and in turn he would love his mother. He would know his land.

Margaret waited for him in her kitchen while warming her hands on the cooling tea pot. By 10:00 a.m. Ray had not arrived. He had no excuse today. There could be no mistaking the park they had planned to enjoy together that morning. Although the park was nameless and not yet an official park, people did not confuse it with any other place.

Ray had promised last night after the farewell party. He had said, "Of course I'll be the one to take you to the park opening. Eight-thirty, kiddo. I can't wait to hear the Zalm play daddy. *Oh, what shall I name you my little park.*" But Ray had mumbled the words through her bedroom door; it was possible that she had not heard him properly. He may have said 10:30. If she hadn't closed the door on him and the visiting grandchildren, insisting that she needed to sleep, maybe there wouldn't be any confusion now.

She had said "Ray?" when she heard him walking away from her bedroom door. "This is the last party we'll have in this house."

"This place is too big for you anyhow," Ray said. "Sitka Lodge—you'll have an easier time of it there."

"I am too old to tend the garden, aren't I?"

He said, "I know." But later she thought he may have said, "So?"

"Then why does selling it feel so wrong?" she asked.

She did not hear his response. She said, "Ray?"

At 10:30 she left her front porch for the stairs. From her garden she saw people walking the genteel shadow-green highway that ran in front of her house—children screaming and running about with popsicles and licorice sticks, mothers with napkins, wiping the orange sugar marks formed around their children's mouths; fathers with infants in packs, jostling the little bodies on their backs as they strode by. She could see them all so well.

Maybe that was why Ray was late. All those children and their mothers swarming the highway. All the pretty mothers that a little girl's eye beholds when her own mother is not beside her, forcing the girl to ask the question from the beginning place of her heart, Where is my Mama right now?

And the girl's father, Margaret's poor son Ray, will have to say, "She's gone to the place all people go."

Katelyn, the youngest of Ray's children, asks, "Where's that, Daddy?" And to the sky, "Where? Right now?"

Ray says, "You know. You know where she is. She's everywhere."

"Like God, right?"

"Like God," he says with the confidence of truth.

At 10:45, meeting up with Ray and his children seemed impossible. Margaret resolved to watch the park opening on TV. She was about to turn inside the house when the trees whispered beside her. Ocean Green, she heard them say. Their colours swayed—the cedar's green, alders, the berry bushes flowering white and pink. Tall grasses and brambles stretched in the wind toward the sunlight blowing east. Ocean Green, she thought. Ocean Green it must be. She had sent thirty entries, all with the same name.

She insisted on the park's name just as she had insisted on Ray's name. After he was born, she had spent four days crying until Charlie agreed to leave the naming up to her. Ray, John, William—it made no discernable difference to Charlie which of these names his son would have. The only part about the naming that bothered him was how Margaret insisted on excluding him. She needed to name the baby herself. Charlie got to give the child its surname, Margaret reasoned, so she should manage the first name. Naming something means it belongs to you and you belong to it. Explorers knew this, she told Charlie. And immigrants, he said. And locals.

She had told Ray the story many times. She had named him by herself. But she went no further; she did not say, And therefore, you are mine. I brought you here. I named you. She did not say the things she meant. Why are you becoming a ghost? I know you have no one, but tell me I still have a son. She could not say it.

In the odd moments of silence, between the cries and laughter of so many children walking along the highway, Margaret discerned a distant rhythmic chanting; undulating voices peaked and fell between the beat of drums. She had not known the opening celebration would host a carnival as well. She stopped listening to her beautiful trees, the drums and chants, and resigned herself to TV images of the park opening. Though she had to admit it: she would be resentful of the screen. If she were to win the naming contest—and she believed there was a reasonable chance of this—she should like to stand on the podium with the various local dignitaries and say it aloud. "Ocean Green. Think of it as your mother."

She had put in her years of letter writing, petitioning to save the trees from men who considered themselves visionaries—who saw miles of buildings, highways, pipelines, more housing. She appealed to them by describing the nurturing effects of the trees, the oxygen they provided, the cradles of fir branches woven together that they formed. In fact she felt especially qualified to win the park-naming contest because of all her letter writing. Ocean Green, she insisted. Ocean Green Park.

It was an ideal name, no one could dispute it. Ocean Green would let no one forget where she or he really was: inside an acreage of trees, certainly, but just down the hill—on the northwest edges of the park—the greenish Pacific swept the sand along Spanish Banks beach, unforgettable.

She had named the trees Ocean Green the year she arrived in Canada and had called them that ever since. On regular mornings she visited the Green and said, You are mine. You are mine. Even her husband Charlie, too, felt compelled to name when they first arrived from England. Their backyard became 'Moss Hollow' through his insistence. For a time she felt she was on someone else's ground—Charlie's—whenever she stepped into the very backyard where she and Charlie had spent days together hunched and aching in admiration of the rich soil, pulling weeds and planting seedlings.

Margaret waited by the tea kettle. She prepared a fourth cup of tea, made from the one-penny bag that she had been pressing hard against the pot every half hour for the last two hours, adding fresh water whenever the pot sat dry. Squeezing tea was one of the few traditions she remembered from her own mother's kitchen in another country which she did her best to forget.

When she did think of it, she mostly recalled the colour of a rose door, and behind it her mother pulling at her brown stocking, bidding goodbye to the owner of the lovely door (a woman in a smart dress, each hair on her head strained to meet the others in a perfect bun). At the bottom of the grand stairs Margaret waited for her mother to receive her week's pay, and then accompanied her toward the grey horizon, toward the station, home.

She stood over the slowly boiling pot, waiting for something to feel right. She wandered into the living room. The image on the screen was of a group of Native men, outfitted in traditional feather headdresses. They were each beating a drum and chanting—their sound was interfering with the voice of the white man speaking into the microphone at the podium.

The camera did not move from the Native men for a long while. Margaret walked to the window and looked longingly for a sign of Ray's car.

You are my ocean green, my sea of possibilities, she had

said to Ray, aged 4½ months, when she found a spread of alders reaching to the sun deep in the nameless acreage near her house. She had been walking through the woods, Baby Ray strapped across her chest. She had wanted these alders to be hers, always, sacred. She had nursed him under their shade for seven months more, until her boy was weaned and the alders had stripped all their leaves. She mothered differently from her mother; she could look her child in the eyes.

She had wanted Ocean Green in the same way she had wanted her mother: all to herself. To own the body that provided, so as to keep and protect it. She could not say it made no difference not to have a mother, a Motherland. She could not console Ray about it. It had always made a difference to her.

Her own mother: Barbara Musson sitting in a dank Fulham kitchen, east London, a charwoman as distant to Margaret as the expensive homes she cleaned. Spotless yet empty, Barbara too had had no land, no earth to grow food. Her own mother, Kate Gordon, dead at 22, by factory fire and Kate's own mother, name unknown, leaving her children a legacy of lacking, a history without land or mothers. Here, Ray and Canada, to change all that. Here, Margaret and Ray in the forest green, soaking up the light pouring through the tree tops, breast to mouth. Here to say you are mine and I am yours. It was not possible with her mother, but with her son there was a chance.

And then there was Charlie's Moss Hollow: the yard full of soft contours that held the family together. The earth rich with memories of Ray running across it, and of her own body kneeling into it. Charlie, smiling between her and Ray, laying a tender moment in the furrows.

Still, she had signed the sale agreement. To the soil that

had held her for years, she said: I relinquish you. As if mothers were expendable. By the wordy mark of her pen: I release you. You are not mine.

The new owners lived in the East and had never touched the land. The real estate agent could not lie, he said. They had bought Margaret's house, one of the oldest in the district, in hopes of replacing it with two Vancouver Specials, the unsightly boxes that had sprung up around the city in various incarnations over the last twenty-five years. Margaret's property, like other unspectacular homes in the neighbourhood, had recently grown obese in value.

She had mentioned to Ray at the farewell party that she did not know if a retirement lodge would provide her with any sustenance.

He had said, "You've always been too sentimental."

She said, "Aren't you?"

And he said, "What I know is that you are too soft."

Sometimes her mother and her son said the same sorts of things. Other times, they held entirely opposite views. Although they had never once met, they each believed that Margaret, as mother and as daughter, was too soft. Her son would say, Face up, you must look life straight in the eyes, no matter how painful it is. Her mother would say, If you look at life too closely you might fall in. Do not be so soft that you feel the bite of anything.

One evening, in the spring of Margaret's tenth year, she had been dallying behind her mother, as she often did, toward the station in Chigwell. The evening light was dark green, and the colour had led Margaret on a long daydream to Eden, imagining what things must have been like there. Along the way, she picked bunches of flowering weeds to the sound of her distant mother calling to hurry up now, march, march, quit dragging your legs, your father needs his supper. Margaret ran finally, tripped over the upside of a road curb and fell smack onto both knees, her hands not breaking the fall because of the bouquet she held.

At first she could not stand. She did not know how to command her legs to move, no less to actually lift her entire body off the ground. Instead she dragged herself to the platform and waited there for the train, telling her mother that she could not stand. That's your own pain, my girl. No need to be sharing it with anyone. You keep it to yourself.

It was not until later that night, when Margaret fell unconscious from the pain, that a doctor was called to diagnose her shattered knee cap. Her mother arranged for three weeks off work and sat at the foot of Margaret's bed, quietly staring out the window in an attempt to care for her.

And then there was Ray. Ray outside the door the night his Susan died. Ray, her beautiful son, his soft brown eyes, his sad mouth, trembling, and Margaret knowing that she did not know how to begin to heal him, or how to even bleed his wound. Susan's death had broken him, and he was in half somehow. He needed his mother to do something as he stood on her doorstep saying it had finally happened. It was all over.

Then he said, Mother, may I come in? And all Margaret could think of was how impossible she was for not bringing him in the house. He had to ask. He had to tell her how to do it, how to handle this death. She was ill-equipped; she did not know what to do with the pain of her own blood, her son.

Young people danced on TV. Kids the same age as Katelyn and her brothers occupied most of the screen, and in the background trees peaked through. Margaret scanned the miniaturized crowd for any sign of her kin.

The cameraman, was he bored? No single image lasted longer than a second or two, and then, on the pavement beneath the stage, the Native men with their drums. An announcer's voice filtered through and said, "In spite of the Band's claim to the spectacular area well-known to Vancouverites, the Premier is presiding over today's event in the fashion of a celebration."

'Green Heart Park' was Katelyn's entry in the park-naming competition. In school Katelyn had seen an aerial photograph of the western tip of Vancouver and decided that the big woods took the shape of a heart. Her teacher had asked how she could see this since the park's shape was clearly rectangular. Katelyn had said if you try hard enough you can see anything.

She had told the story last night at the farewell party, and Margaret had been instantly depressed by it.

Ray and the children had joined together in her house for the last time, last night. They had come with a prepared supper. Margaret sat down to their meal of new potatoes, glazed ham, fresh greens, and cabbage cooked in ginger marmalade, but she could not eat. She said to Ray, "What if the new owners build a carport over Moss Hollow?"

Ray pulled at his beard, twisted strands together, unravelled them, then started over. He spoke quietly to Katelyn, who appeared to prefer playing under the coffee table to being outside with her brothers.

"Did you say something, Mother?" He passed her a plate of

sliced cucumber soaking in cider vinegar. He said, "Don't starve yourself."

She said, "I'll miss my trees when I move."

He said, "Of course you will. They're your family."

"Thank you," she said.

Ray never lied. He told the children how and why their mother had died. He told them that their Nana talked to trees and it did not mean she was crazy. Beside a certain red cedar Margaret spoke with Charlie, long since gone. She heard voices in the brush and saw God between the trees in the form of dew bearded on a spider's web. Although Ray didn't know it, she also had conversations there with him, and in those conversations Ray told her that she had been an excellent mother.

Sometimes Margaret spoke in the woods to Susan, Ray's lost wife, mother to Katelyn and the boys, daughter-in-law, part-time grade 9 teacher, gardener, origami bird maker and downhill skier with thick long hair that she pulled across her soft face whenever she wanted to laugh and hide it, girlish, playful, tanned arms and soft lips she'd place on Ray's neck.

How does he live without you? Margaret asked. Who will those children go to when they want only you, you, you? You were a girl, no matter how old you might have become. You were a girl, my dear, to the end.

Katelyn put her plate of ham on the coffee table and undid Margaret's shoes.

"What are these balls on your toes, Nana?" Katelyn said. "Our mother didn't have them."

Margaret said, "They're only for us old gals."

"So if my mom had got old she'd have these balls, too?"

"Not necessarily, dear. How about a ginger ale?"

"Naw," Katelyn said. "No thank you. Did my mom wear shoes like yours?"

Ray said, "Your Mother had huge long feet, Katie. They were as narrow as could be and her second toe was her biggest."

"Like mine?" Katelyn asked.

"Just like yours," Ray said, and Katelyn smiled.

Margaret had no part in it. She was incapable of talking without tears about Susan. But Ray would talk to anyone about her. "The speech act is the most important act." Ray said that constantly. He needed to talk every day about her death. And he reasoned that he could access friends and neighbours more easily than he could afford to talk to a therapist.

He often spoke with other mothers in the park. The mothers might be pushing their babies on the swings, and Ray would strike up a conversation about Susan, how she died, how he had quit everything—his job and his night school to become a full time parent. The life insurance would stretch seven years he figured. He was even talking about home-schooling.

Margaret learned about Ray's life by listening to him in playgrounds. There was never any lack of mothers, with widened eyes and dropped mouths, who, upon hearing of Susan's death by cancer, would look ever so lovingly at their own children coming down the high slide, and who would later leave the park hugging those children tighter than on any other day.

The family tradition hadn't continued; Ray was a mother. The line of unmothered mothers—who knows how long— ended with Ray. He was as soft as the earth, too.

"But these kids need a home, Ray," Margaret said, as she often did. "I'm selling so you can give it to them."

WOMAN WITH A MAN INSIDE

"Mother, please. They have one. They have me. That'll have to do."

"I want to speak to you in my kitchen, Ray."

Ray looked down. "Say whatever it is in front of her."

Margaret looked at Katelyn, who was pretending not to listen. She was stroking the socks on her feet.

"The kitchen, Ray," she said.

"I'm a big girl, Nana."

"Your father insists you are."

Ray said, "Mother, the kitchen."

Ray sat beside Margaret in the kitchen. She wanted to hold his hand, but could not. "You cannot identify with your kids, Ray, because I am your mother and I am alive."

Ray said, "Very."

"I know what it means to be without a mother. I know how much you can love your land."

Ray said, "I really don't believe that buying a house or land or whatever will help them to have a mother. Is that what you're trying to say?"

Yes, somehow, that is what she meant. He did not understand her. Everything around her had begun to reflect how she was evaporating, like breath on a mirror. Every year Ray aged he became less recognizable as someone who had lived in her body. At one time she felt that she had birthed all her grandchildren, too. She remembered the way each child had behaved as a baby in Moss Hollow. Ray had always been passive and happy. Katelyn had howled all day.

Ray said, "Your job is done, Mother."

Katelyn yelled, "I'll be on the porch," and ran out the back door, singing "fighting and biting, I'd rather go...kiting." Margaret heard her grandsons piling in through the door just after Katelyn left. She could hear the boys clamouring on top of each other, fighting to get into the living room first, each yelling claims to a bowl of brownie frosting.

Margaret said, "Maybe it's time to pack it in." And she left Ray in the kitchen.

The boys ate with their fingers and tongues. They swarmed around the dining-room table, piled slices of cucumber onto leftover bread rolls, and ate Margaret's portion of ham. They did handstands against the walls. Margaret stood in front of the window and stared onto her garden. Ray had his arm around Katelyn in Moss Hollow.

Saucers full of half-eaten pickles and beets lay about the house. Scrunched napkins waited for her attention. Cubes of ice patiently melted in glasses. The farewell party, although it had barely started, was waning.

Charlie would never have understood what the world had become or how Ray had to live. She raised a shoulder away from her grandchildren, refusing to savour, or even taste, their last visit. Suddenly these children were not her kin. None of these creatures had been a baby swaying in Moss Hollow. She did not recognize any of them. None would visit her at the retirement lodge.

Margaret took herself up the stairs, closed her bedroom door and lay on the bed. The moon hung between two branches as it had done a thousand times before. The thin curtains permitted light into the room, the light full and quiet.

She felt a tightening in her throat.

When Ray came to the door she tried to make her voice sound relaxed, without congestion. She said, "It's past my

WOMAN WITH A MAN INSIDE

bedtime."

He did not press her to open the door as she expected. "We're family, Ray," Margaret said.

She could not hear her son. He appeared not to have said anything. *Thank you. Thank you.* Why could she not hear those words. Why would he never say them?

"Say goodbye to the children for me," Margaret said.

She listened to him go down the stairs.

She listened to him doing as she had instructed, the children zipping their coats, thudding down the front stairs, the door locking into place, car engine revving, the noise of it accelerating into the distance. Then the fast whine of a bicyclist's spokes speeding through the wind.

She listened to nothing for a long time. An hour passed without sleep. She surrendered to the insomnia and went downstairs to the kitchen. Traces of the party were left: root-beer bottles lined against the back door, the frosting bowl with impressions in the skin of remaining chocolate, a box of crackers and the toaster. The counters shone. Mother would lose. Ocean Green would lose. She knew it then.

In her best copper-bottomed pot, she heated milk, slowly. This place might not remember her. She stirred. The trees, the garden, Susan, so young. Canada. England. She could be forgotten entirely. She stopped stirring, turned the milk down just before it reached a boil.

More men in feather headdresses appeared from the trails leading out of the forest. Margaret looked dimly for Ray and Katelyn, wanting to hold them, to touch her own people, to apologize for something.

"And then they want the land back, or as they prefer to say, they want to be returned to the land," the TV announcer said.

Along the stage huge banners flapped red, white and blue—the reigning party's colours. It was all so unfamiliar, she could have been watching the American news. She could have been anywhere on the continent.

The chanting grew louder and stormed the attempted words of a woman who stood at the front of the stage, behind the podium, vainly smiling at the microphone before her. Oversized speakers conspired in complete domination at each end of the podium, but the woman at the microphone couldn't be heard. The drumming and other unofficial sounds were being picked up, it seemed, by the microphones on stage.

Officials sat in rows behind the speakers.

The words "Musqueam, Musqueam" pulsed through the speakers, rapid and in unison with the drums' beat. "Musqueam. Musqueam." More Natives in traditional dress came onto the screen. Each carried a drum; each chanted at the same pitch and speed. "MUSQUEAM." The camera panned the crowd. Margaret could not tell where sympathies lay. As usual, the white residents of the district were too polite to divide into camps. Their politics were more subtle, betrayed only by the kind of smile they might give, the glaze of their eyes, the nodding of their heads, their postures.

Then Ray tapped her on the shoulder. "Mother, I've been calling at you for an entire minute." Ray stood in her living room, and Katelyn clung to the front door, two dolls and baby bottles tucked under her arms.

"Where are the boys?" Margaret asked.

"I dropped them at the celebration."

"Where were you?"

"Katelyn fell out of a tree this morning. I took her to the doctor. Just a bruise in the end."

"What's happening, Ray?"

"Happy and Sarah wanted their mom today. They went to the doctor, too."

Katelyn held onto Ray's hand. "Nana, you look sick."

"I feel fine, dear," Margaret said, turning slightly to the TV.

The Premier stood at the podium holding an envelope while the commotion from the speakers pushed into the congregation. Some people pulled back their children as the Natives drummed faster, chanting "MUSQUEAM."

Katelyn said, "Nana, why don't you sit down?"

The Premier continued to smile. His teeth looked too big for his head. The officials behind him directed their smiles, like reinforcements, at him. He spoke into the microphone, but no one could hear him. He smiled wider.

"Do you think I'm going to win, Nana?"

Margaret asked, "Win what?"

"Green Heart Park."

"It can always be that to you."

Ray glanced at the TV and said, "There's not a chance for them."

The wind had died, and the trees were blue in the stillness. The Premier opened the envelope. Some people yelled the Premier's name and clapped for him. "Go, Bill, Go, Bill, Go Zalm."

The Premier read the name from the envelope.

"MUSQUEAM, MUSQUEAM" was all anyone could hear from the speakers.

"Feedback," Ray said. "Somehow they're making their words feed-back through the stage speakers."

The Premier's mouth moved; repeated the name and smiled; repeated the name three, then four times, and smiled.

"MUSQUEAM, MUSQUEAM."

"Is it true?" she said, wanting to hold Ray's hand now, wanting it to be true. It held more hope than Ocean Green. If the Premier said Musqueam, then there would be proof— proof that it was possible to be returned to something that has left you, or has been taken from you. Mother, son, your Native land, your life. How long it had been since she had touched her sun ray.

The amplified sounds were suddenly lost, their power cut.

The Premier yelled the name into the anxious congregation.

The TV announcer said, "The official name is travelling through the crowd by word of mouth. I've just received confir-mation. We're now standing in Pacific Spirit Park. That's the winning entry as submitted by Miss Sherry Sakamoto."

A young Japanese woman took the stage.

Ray did not look at his mother. He listened to the analysis that followed. Katelyn walked out the back door. She sat with her dolls on a branch of the plum. She rocked herself to the rhythm of an unrecognizable lullaby.

Margaret neared her.

"Make a mama, make a daddy who's a mama…" Katelyn brushed back the hair of one doll and fussed a bottle into the other's mouth. She made more words with the passing seconds. "Here or there…There or here. Keep on looking everywhere."